BEFORE A FALL

A Pride and Prejudice Reimagining

JENNIFER KAY

for Debbie

CHAPTER ONE

Elizabeth Bennet hated being female. Oh, normally it wasn't all that bad. Skirts were less practical than trousers and she could certainly never dream of going to Cambridge, but she found it easy to laugh off or ignore most of the inconveniences that came with being one of the fairer sex. This was different.

He hadn't even let her say no! The one thing she had thought within her power—the right to accept or reject a marriage proposal—had been brushed aside as an 'established custom of her sex!' The nerve of the man! And *such* a proposal! Let her cousin think she was displaying feminine delicacy, let her mother wail until the end of time— she, Elizabeth, would never be Mrs. Collins. She would not even go back to Longbourn until he left.

Therein lay another problem with being female. Where else could she go? She did not ride and had no horse in any case. She commanded no carriage. Elizabeth considered Lucas Lodge briefly, but dismissed it. Word would reach Longbourn of where she had gone almost immediately—better to go home directly than seek refuge with Charlotte Lucas. Her aunt Phillips in Meryton would be worse still. Spend a night out of doors or attempt to hide elsewhere nearby and her reputation would be in tatters. Sick as she was of men, Elizabeth did not particularly care for the effect it would have on herself, but Jane! She could not stand if her actions ruined Jane's chances with Mr. Bingley.

That left one option, and certainly not an ideal one: her aunt and uncle Gardiner in London, twenty-four miles away. "A horse, a horse, my kingdom for a horse," Elizabeth muttered to herself. She looked up, taking in her surroundings blankly. Even for a young lady who walked far more than proper, twenty-four miles may as well have been twenty score. *And* by running off with no plan, she'd covered over a mile—away from London. It was hopeless.

Elizabeth sighed. At least she'd had the sense to skirt around Meryton instead of going through it. Word wouldn't have spread into the town yet, but there was no use in giving people more fodder for gossip. She looked around, smiling slightly at the sight of her muddied boots and hem. Her would-be fiancé wouldn't dare follow her through the muck, at least. Sighing again, she turned back in the direction she had been heading and kept going. As her anger began to cool, she could see how ridiculous it was to not go home. But… *Not yet. Just not yet.*

She walked on in silence for a time, her eyes on the toes of her boots. Surely her father would support her. He, who had laughed at Mr. Collins since the first seconds of his visit, could not force her into a marriage with the man! Even if her mother insisted, she could count on an ally in her father, couldn't she? Maybe—no. Better not to think.

Lost in the turmoil of her own thoughts, Elizabeth nearly failed to recognize the voices ahead of her. Then a flash of red caught her eye as a man in an officer's jacket moved across an opening in the line of trees and she stopped short, blinking as she made sense of her surroundings. Had she really walked the whole way to Netherfield? It seemed impossible, but Elizabeth was certain she recognized the trees ahead as the edge of Netherfield's park. She'd walked that path often during her stay with the Bingleys.

The man crossed the gap again and her heart leapt. Mr. Wickham would be just the person to remind her that not all men were horrible, grasping creatures. Elizabeth opened her mouth to call out and stopped as she took in his manner. He was agitated, angry. And who was he talking to? Not Mr. Darcy, surely?

Curiosity getting the better of her, Elizabeth crept forward towards the thickest part of the trees, where the branches created an almost solid wall. Peering through a small hole in her cover, she could just make out Mr. Wickham's companion. It was not Mr. Darcy, a fact that rather disappointed Elizabeth. No, the subject of Wickham's agitation was a young lady that Elizabeth had never seen before. The lady's face was nearly as white as her gown, and she stood with her arms wrapped tightly around her middle, watching Wickham with more than a little trepidation.

Mr. Wickham frightening someone? It was completely opposite of what she knew of the man, although Elizabeth had to admit that his manner was remarkably different than when she had interacted with him. And, if she was completely honest with herself, how well could she really know the man? After all, she'd met him just a week ago. But still…

Elizabeth forced her attention back to the scene before her in time to see the lady take a step back as Wickham approached her. He grabbed both her arms in response.

"Surely you must see reason, *Miss Darcy*," he snarled. "No one will want ruined goods, no matter how much money comes with them."

"I am not ruined goods!" Miss Darcy—*Miss Darcy!* —protested, her words punctuated with struggles as she tried to free herself from his grip.

"Oh, but that can change," Wickham responded, pulling her closer despite her attempts to escape.

"And you'd be happy to take the money, wouldn't you? You wouldn't be here if it wasn't for the money."

Wickham actually laughed. "The money should have been mine already, Georgiana. We were so close last year. If not for your damned brother—"

"My brother saved me!" she burst out.

"Yes, and therein lies the other appeal of truly ruining you. I can't wait to see his face when he realizes my revenge." One hand suddenly went to her shoulder, grabbing the neckline of her dress and yanking. Georgiana gave a strangled cry and struggled harder. "Too bad your dear brother isn't here to, ah, *save* you again," Wickham sneered.

Elizabeth had seen enough. However awful Mr. Darcy had been, Mr. Wickham seemed far worse at the moment. Even if he *had* been denied a living and cast out penniless by the brother, it was no excuse to treat the sister in such a horrid way. Almost before she registered her actions, Elizabeth had snatched up a fist-sized rock from the ground and moved to the gap in the trees.

Miss Darcy's eyes widened, and Wickham instinctively glanced over his shoulder, then did a double take when he recognized her. "Miss Elizabeth!" he exclaimed, his normal charming look crossing his face and then faltering as he took in her expression. "Miss Darcy and I were just, uh—"

She didn't wait to hear whatever excuse he would stutter out, but pulled back her arm and let the rock fly, praying that her aim hadn't deteriorated so much as to hit the young lady instead of her target. She'd perfected rock throwing the summer she was nine, but even her father, with his lax sense of propriety, had discouraged that activity as she grew older.

To Lizzy's relief the rock *thunked* satisfactorily against Mr. Wickham's head. It wasn't a perfect hit—glancing against his temple rather than smashing his nose as Elizabeth had hoped—but still hard enough that he released Miss Darcy and staggered back a step, yelping. Before he could retaliate, Elizabeth scooped up another rock and flung it at his midsection. She was going for a third when he turned and ran, disappearing down a trail back into the park.

In the sudden silence, the two young ladies stood staring at each other, both breathing hard and trembling. Then Miss Darcy collapsed onto the stone path and started sobbing. For several moments, Elizabeth just stared, trying to make sense of what she had witnessed.

Miss Darcy's presence was incidental—Caroline Bingley had likely written to invite her the moment that Mr. Bingley seemed taken with Jane, for hadn't Caroline hinted that she intended for her brother to marry Miss Darcy? Mr. Wickham's behavior, though, was irreconcilable with the man that Elizabeth had talked to and admired. Were all men truly so selfish? Mr. Collins only talking about his own desires and expectations as he proposed, Wickham ruining a girl for money and revenge, Darcy refusing to talk or dance with anyone because they didn't meet his precious standards, even her own father hiding in his study and only emerging to laugh at her mother. Well, fine! She was *done* with men.

Elizabeth clenched her fists, then yelped as the rock she still held sliced her hand. She dropped the rock and examined her hand indifferently, bending to wipe the blood on her hem. Now she'd have mud *and* blood on her skirts. Well, her mother couldn't be much more upset with her at this point, and she couldn't do anything about it now. She might however, be able to help the upset girl on the other side of the trees.

Her skirt caught and tore as Elizabeth pushed through the dense row of trees; she ignored it. Settling herself down on the path several feet from the still-sobbing Miss Darcy, she took the chance to observe the girl.

Miss Darcy had her brother's dark hair and perhaps his eyes, but that was where the similarities ended. She was slender and no taller than Elizabeth herself, with delicate features. Of course, Miss Darcy was only fifteen or sixteen—Elizabeth forgot which—and might gain some of her brother's height in time. Having expected a younger Caroline Bingley, vain and aloof, Elizabeth was surprised at how very, well, human this girl seemed. Part of it was the circumstances, but the conversation Elizabeth had overheard made it clear that there had been more to Miss Darcy's life than drawing pictures and practicing piano.

"Please, you mustn't...you mustn't think that," Miss Darcy started without looking up.

"That you somehow encouraged that horrid display of manners?" Elizabeth asked matter-of-factly. "Of course I don't."

Miss Darcy glanced up, face half hidden behind her hair. "But you don't know me, you might," she stopped, looking utterly terrified, and for the first time it occurred to Elizabeth that Miss Darcy could have been truly ruined if someone inclined to gossip had come upon the scene rather than herself. Wickham was known and generally liked, and this girl was the sister of the proud and unpopular Mr. Darcy. There were some—her sister Lydia came to mind—who would take his side no matter what the truth of it was.

"I might nothing," Elizabeth replied firmly. "Besides, I've had my own awful experience with a man today." When Miss Darcy's eyes widened in surprise, she smiled wryly. "Well, I saw your experience. It's only fair I tell you mine. I'm Elizabeth, by the way. Miss Elizabeth Bennet, but I usually go by Lizzy. You must be Mr. Darcy's sister."

"Yes," Miss Darcy said rather hesitantly, "Miss Georgiana. I wish I had a shorter nickname, but I don't. I like the name Lizzy."

"And I like the name Georgiana," Elizabeth said. "Please, call me Lizzy."

The younger girl looked up and gave her a brief but brilliant smile before her face dropped back into anxiousness.

"Right," Elizabeth said. "My own experience with an abhorrent man began not long after breakfast this morning." She recounted the entirety of his proposal, putting as much humor in the story as she could. It was easier to do since having seen Wickham's viciousness. Mr. Collins hadn't assaulted her, at least, and his astounding officiousness may distract Georgiana from her own experience, if only for a while. Scooting closer to Georgiana, she leaned against her lightly as she continued to tell the tale, and after a few moments, Georgiana shifted her own weight back against Elizabeth and dropped her head onto Lizzy's shoulder.

Cradling her hand in her lap so as not to reopen the cut, Elizabeth continued to talk about light-hearted things, telling Georgiana of her desire to escape to London and inventing wild plans for how she might accomplish the trip. Only when she paused for breath did the voice in the back of her mind fill her mind.

Dear Lord, how in the world did I end up here?

CHAPTER TWO

Mr. Darcy found them like that some time later. He came striding down the path with a thunderous look on his face, which turned to incredulity as he stopped short at the sight of them. Elizabeth sighed inwardly, resigning herself to the certain unpleasantness. Georgiana burst into fresh tears.

At her outburst, his face softened, and he knelt in front of her, taking her shoulders in his big hands. "Did he hurt you, Georgiana?" he asked tersely, and Elizabeth could hear that he was fighting back rage.

His sister shook her head mutely and seemed to tuck herself in to be even smaller. Then she burst out, "I did not—please, Fitzwilliam, I promise, I didn't... I didn't know he was here, I," she choked to a stop. "No, he didn't hurt me, but Lizzy, her hand, she made him go away and it cut her hand." She stopped and stared down, tears dripping into her lap.

Mr. Darcy had flinched at the use of her nickname, and he looked to her now, mutely asking for an explanation. She shrugged and held out her hand, palm up. The bleeding had stopped, but blood had dried over half of her hand, giving it a garish appearance. "It is not so bad as it looks, I only need to clean it," she said calmly.

Mr. Darcy blinked slowly once, twice, and then met Elizabeth's gaze again. "And how did you come to cut your hand in the first place?" he enquired.

Elizabeth had intended to meet him calmly in every manner, if only for Georgiana's sake, but the intensity of his stare made her drop her eyes. Still, she managed to say lightly, "Oh, one of the rocks I picked up had a sharp edge, and I was not so careful as I ought to have been."

There was another pause before he queried, "*One* of the rocks?"

She forced herself to meet his eyes again and said frankly, "Yes, sir, there are rather a large number of them on the other side of those trees. I picked up three in all. Have you ever noticed what good projectiles rocks make in times of need?"

His jaw dropped. "You—"

"Threw two rocks at Mr. Wickham, yes. The first hit his head, the second, his stomach. The third cut me. I dropped it over there," she gestured, "if you would like to assess the sharpness for yourself."

"I will take your word for it," he said. "Georgiana, can you stand?"

His sister looked up at him without moving. "How did you know where I was?"

"Miss Bingley told me you had arrived and gone for a walk, and when I came to find you I saw that—" he stopped, clenching his teeth. "I saw Mr.

Wickham leaving the park. I was understandably concerned." His eyes flicked to Elizabeth. "The fact that he was holding his head did confuse me at the time."

"Will he come back?" Georgiana asked anxiously.

"It matters not," Darcy responded. When both Georgiana and Elizabeth gasped, he continued, "We leave tomorrow. He must stay with his regiment or risk being hanged as a deserter." His voice softened slightly. "You need not worry, Georgie."

Taking the opportunity to lighten the conversation, Elizabeth elbowed Georgiana lightly. "And here I thought you said you had no shorter nicknames," she teased.

"Only William calls me Georgie," the girl whispered.

The use of his Christian name surprised Elizabeth, and she glanced up at the man. He stood looking down at his sister with a resigned look on his face. "Come, Georgiana," he said in a tired voice.

Most likely Mr. Darcy wished his sister *was* more like a young Caroline Bingley, Elizabeth thought as she watched the exchange. Men! Were any of them capable of seeing women as more than objects? Careful not to use her injured hand, she pushed herself to her feet, then turned to offer a hand to Georgiana, who took it without meeting her eyes. Once standing, Georgiana immediately wrapped one arm around her middle and used the other to hold the torn neckline of her dress in place. Glancing down at her own torn and dirtied gown, Elizabeth could only imagine the sight they must be.

Suddenly, Darcy turned to her. "How exactly did you come to be here with your rocks, Miss Elizabeth?"

For the first time in her life, Elizabeth had no idea what to say. Mr. Darcy was the last person in the world she would have chosen to tell about Mr. Collins' disastrous proposal. Telling Georgiana had made the event seem—almost—humorous. Confide in Mr. Darcy, and he would have yet more reason to disdain her family, as if last night's ball hadn't given him enough reason for a lifetime. Then again, there was something freeing about facing a person whose good opinion was all but irretrievable.

As Elizabeth struggled with her thoughts, she glanced up and found Georgiana watching her with sympathy. She looked utterly cowed and resigned. Goodness knows what kind of scolding Mr. Darcy had planned for his sister once they were in private. Very well, she would do what she could to shift his focus to her relatives rather than his own.

"I received a proposal of marriage this morning, Mr. Darcy," Elizabeth said evenly.

14

"And did that proposal take place in Bingley's park?" he inquired coolly, one eyebrow raising. "Bingley himself seemed rather more taken with your sister, and he left for London several hours ago in any case."

Elizabeth registered a flash of regret for Jane, followed by an equal amount of surprise that Mr. Darcy seemed to have attempted a joke. Then he went on, "I do not know of any other gentlemen—"

He stopped abruptly, eyes widening and then narrowing in suspicion. Their conversation about Mr. Wickham the previous night came back to her in a rush. She'd made it rather obvious which man she preferred. A dangerous look crossed Darcy's face and he opened his mouth, but she cut him off.

"I believe you met my cousin, Mr. Collins, yesterday evening. It was he who proposed this morning, sir, and certainly not in Mr. Bingley's garden."

"Mr. Collins." Darcy said the name as if he had never heard it before, frowning even more than he had been before. "Your father's estate is entailed on him, I believe?"

"It is, sir."

"Then this must be a great relief for your family."

Why did he keep staring at her like that? Surely that couldn't be *pity*. Not from the grand Mr. Darcy.

"I am sure it would be, but I did not accept the proposal."

His eyebrows rose again, and she noticed how expressive his face was when not locked into a scowl or indifference. "You did not accept him?"

"Yes, I believe you could say I rejected him, if that terminology suits you better."

She swore the hint of a smile crossed Mr. Darcy's face. "And I suppose that is a good enough reason for your presence here. Mr. Collins deserves my pity, but I cannot deny I am glad that you had reason to walk farther than you normally would."

What? He was capable of recognizing feelings in another human being? Well, the feelings were wasted on Mr. Collins. "Do not worry, Mr. Darcy. Mr. Collins is far more concerned with Lady Catherine's regard than with mine."

"Then he is more of a fool than I gave him credit for, and I did not think that possible," he replied.

For the second time that day, Elizabeth was rendered speechless. She looked up at Mr. Darcy blankly, struggling to find a comeback—*any* comeback, let alone a witty one. At that moment, though, Georgiana gave a great sneeze and shivered. Immediately, Mr. Darcy's attention transferred back to his sister. He removed his jacket and draped it around her shoulders, covering the tear in her dress and providing more warmth than the gown did. Elizabeth had started to notice the chilly air herself, especially since she was neither walking nor warmed with anger, and she wrapped her arms around herself. He must have noticed, for he directed his words to both ladies as he steered Georgiana down the path.

"Let's go inside where it is warmer. There is a back entrance that should avoid the attention of, ah, the household."

Caroline Bingley, Elizabeth thought to herself.

"Miss Elizabeth, I am sure we can find someone to tend to your hand and," he looked her over once again, "perhaps another dress for you to wear."

She considered refusing his invitation, but the alternative was returning home in a sorry state. Here was an excuse to avoid the impending storm of her mother for the afternoon. Surely an afternoon with the Darcy's at Netherfield, imposing as the thought was, couldn't be worse than her mother in a fit of nerves. Smiling wryly to herself, she gave a slight shake of her head and followed the siblings towards the house.

CHAPTER THREE

Elizabeth was astounded when they managed to reach Georgiana's room without setting off a commotion. They had been seen by at least three maids and a footman, and yet not a single one had done more than bob a curtsey or bow and silently return to their duties. Even when Elizabeth had turned to double check, none of them had disappeared to whisper the news into an employer's ear as they would have done at Longbourn.

She was not naïve—Elizabeth was fully aware the servants could simply be more discreet about tattling than she was used to—but her gut told her that was not the case. Either her mother's bad habits had encouraged the Longbourn staff into less professional behavior, or the Netherfield servants were none too loyal to their new master. Contemplating this idea as she followed the Darcys down the final hallway, Elizabeth realized that while Mr. Bingley himself may have inspired confidence and loyalty in his staff, Caroline Bingley was not the type of mistress to do so. And Mr. Bingley was currently gone.

A maid was moving dresses from a trunk to the clothespress when they entered, and she turned to stare. "Miss Georgiana! What happened? Are you hurt?"

"I am fine, thank you," Georgiana replied quietly.

"My sister will require a new dress," Mr. Darcy said.

"Yes—yes, of course, sir," the maid stammered, looking around at the dresses she had been unpacking. She turned back to them and held up the one she was still holding. "Will this do, miss?"

Elizabeth had been watching Georgiana rather than the maid, so she caught the slight wrinkle in the other girl's nose at the sight of the dress. Turning to Mr. Darcy, she said firmly, "Thank you, sir, for seeing us here without incident. Perhaps it would be best to leave this part to us females. We shall find you once the appropriate changes in attire have been made."

For a moment, she thought he would argue, but he simply nodded once and turned on his heel to leave. Looking back, he glanced at Elizabeth and then his sister. "Georgiana, perhaps you could find a dress for Miss Elizabeth as well. She has clearly been through some sort of struggle, and we do not need more rumors than there will be already." Not waiting for an answer, he left.

A strong desire came over Elizabeth to yank the door back open and ask just who he was to order her life for her, but common sense said he was right. The state of her dress would cause considerably more talk than her surprise appearance at Netherfield, and that would be bad enough. She stifled a sigh and focused her attention back on Georgiana.

"I believe, Georgiana, that after the events of this morning we ought to be able to be honest with each other, wouldn't you agree?" Georgiana nodded, and Elizabeth continued, "Then I must insist that you tell me the reason for your dislike of this gown. Is it outdated? Not cut right? I am a simple country miss, and rarely have the chance to hear opinions from fine Town ladies such as yourself."

Georgiana giggled. "Oh, no, Lizzy. The dress is certainly fashionable, and cut well. It's just," she paused and looked to the side as if about to divulge a horrible secret, "I hate stripes. Not on other people!" she hastened to add, noting the stripes on Elizabeth's ruined dress. "But for myself, I have never been able to stand them. I do not know why. That dress would suit you, though. You take that, if you think it will fit; I have several others that will do."

"Georgiana, I couldn't possibly—"

"Please," the younger girl cut her off. "You will be doing me a favor. If you do not wear that dress, then no one will, and it will go out of fashion without ever being used. I do hate wasting things."

"Alright," Elizabeth acquiesced. "Although perhaps I should tend to my hand before I change. I wouldn't want to get blood on a brand new dress."

As she was speaking, the door opened and a second maid appeared, carrying a pitcher of water and a length of linen. "Excuse me, miss and miss, but I was told one of you needed an injury tended."

Elizabeth raised an eyebrow at Georgiana.

Georgiana shrugged. "William is very thoughtful," she said simply.

'William' is very controlling, Elizabeth thought to herself. Aloud, she said, "That would be me. I cut my hand." Holding it out for inspection, she added, "It is not so bad as it looks, but it will need to be cleaned and bandaged before I can change." She may care little about dirtying her own dresses, but she would not cause any harm to Georgiana's loaned gown if she could help it.

The cut, which indeed looked far less dramatic once the dried blood was washed away, was soon bandaged. In less than an hour, the bandage was the only sign that anything out of the ordinary had ever happened, aside from Elizabeth's presence. Unconcerned as she was with the opinions of Miss Bingley and Mr. and Mrs. Hurst, she did not worry what her reception would be. Her main feeling on the matter was curiosity to see how they would react, especially Miss Bingley. Would the servants or Mr. Darcy have alerted them of her presence, or would it be a surprise?

"Have you thought of an appropriate explanation for how we met?" Elizabeth asked Georgiana as the maid put the final touches on Georgiana's hair.

"Oh," Georgiana replied, turning slightly to face Elizabeth. "No, it hadn't occurred to me. I've been trying to avoid thinking about this morning, to be honest. I hadn't thought to ever see…" she trailed off.

Good, Elizabeth thought, walking over to look out the window. *Mention names as little as possible, especially with a maid I don't know right here.* "Let's keep it simple. We were both on a walk when we crossed paths. Miss Bingley and Mrs. Hurst are acquainted with my love of walking and think me quite wild for it, so they shouldn't question that explanation. We began talking and," she stopped, trying to come up with an innocent reason of why she was now in Georgiana's room, wearing one of her dresses.

"And Miss Elizabeth tripped and fell, cutting her hand and ruining her dress," Mr. Darcy said from the doorway. "Since Netherfield was far closer than Longbourn or even your aunt's house in Meryton," he inclined his head towards Elizabeth, "Georgiana insisted you come here."

Georgiana gasped. "And then you could go with us to London tomorrow!"

Elizabeth turned to Georgiana, momentarily forgetting her annoyance at Darcy's intrusion. "That is very kind of you, but I feel as though I have trespassed on your hospitality enough already."

"You would be doing me another favor," Georgiana said. "Mrs. Annesley—my companion—usually travels with me, but she is away to visit a sick sister. Miss Bingley and Mrs. Hurst will likely ride with Mr. Hurst, and so I will have no one to talk to if you do not come."

"Surely Mr. Darcy will not desert you if you wish for company," Elizabeth said, although how Mr. Darcy could make for good company, she couldn't imagine.

"I will ride," Darcy said shortly. "Your presence would not be a problem if you wish to go with us."

"I do not have anything to take with me. I left home rather… suddenly," Elizabeth finished awkwardly.

"No matter," Darcy said. "Send a letter to one of your sisters to pack what you need. We can pick it up as we pass Longbourn tomorrow." With that, he turned and exited the room as abruptly as he had appeared.

"Well," Elizabeth said, staring after him. "Do you really not mind, Georgiana?"

"Oh, no!" Georgiana exclaimed. "It will be such fun to travel with another young lady, and have a friend to visit in Town. I do not—" she stopped short, turning slightly pink.

Elizabeth had no trouble imagining the rest of the sentence. *I do not have many friends.* Was that in London specifically, or overall? Knowing Mr. Darcy, there were few young ladies good enough to be friends with his precious sister. She certainly wouldn't have qualified under normal circumstances. Perhaps he thought the best way to keep her from gossiping about the scene with Mr. Wickham was to treat her as a friend, for surely he considered the friendship of the great Darcy's a sufficient incentive. Officious, insufferable man! She would go with them for true affection for Miss Darcy, not because she could be bought.

"In that case, I have no option but to go," Elizabeth smiled, leading the way out of the room. Thinking of the logistics, she frowned. A note to Jane would ensure that her trunk was packed and waiting. Elizabeth did not think her father would protest to her impromptu journey, but she would make sure to include a passage for him when she wrote her sister. If Mr. Bennet did not approve, she would find out in the morning. Aloud, she said "I ought to send my aunt Gardiner a letter so they are aware of my coming, as well as one to Jane."

They were on the stairs by then, and Georgiana stopped to turn and smile at her. "Of course," Georgiana said brightly. "I am sure Miss Bingley would be happy to lend you her writing supplies." As they descended the rest of the stairs to the drawing room, however, Georgiana seemed to shrink slightly. She had been leading, but by the time they reached the door she was a full step behind Elizabeth, shoulders hunched slightly and hands clasped tightly in front of herself. It was up to Elizabeth to take the first step into a room where she knew that none of the inhabitants would be remotely happy to see her.

"Eliza!" Caroline Bingley exclaimed as they entered the drawing room, startled into standing. She gaped for a moment, then seemed to realize how unbecoming that expression was. Turning away, Miss Bingley made her way across the room towards the window, peering out briefly as if she had meant to stand all along. Had the movement not taken her far closer to Mr. Darcy, Elizabeth might have found the ruse believable. As it was, she stifled a smile. Miss Bingley was welcome to Mr. Darcy and all his arrogant tendencies.

Speaking of his arrogant tendencies, he had apparently neglected to inform Miss Bingley and the Hursts of her presence. Arching one eyebrow at him, she decided that two could play at this game. "Hello, Miss Bingley," she turned slightly, "Mrs. Hurst." She looked for Mr. Hurst, and found him snoring in an armchair in the corner. Looking back at the sisters, she smiled as sweetly as she could manage. "I see Mr. Darcy neglected to inform you that I would be joining your party this afternoon."

Caroline's head snapped towards Mr. Darcy, eyes narrowing slightly. She laughed shortly. "He most certainly did. I am sure, Mr. Darcy, that you have far more important things to think about than the females of your party for a mere afternoon— other than our dear Miss Georgiana, of course."

"Forgive me, Miss Bingley, for my oversight," Mr. Darcy said quietly. He looked as though he would go on, but then simply turned back to studying the room's meager selection of books.

Caroline would not accept his silence. "Are you not relived, Mr. Darcy, to be returning to Town tomorrow? I do find the society there so much more invigorating."

Tired of standing awkwardly in the doorway, Elizabeth moved across the room and sat down at the small table where a chess board was perpetually set up in preparation for a game. Mr. Darcy and Mr. Bingley had played several times during the time Elizabeth had spent at Netherfield. She picked up a white knight and examined the intricate details of the carving. In a move she found ironic, Mr. Darcy always played as white and Bingley as black.

Caroline had not paused in her attempts to engage Mr. Darcy in conversation. "I must confess I even look forward to the carriage ride," Caroline was saying as Georgiana sat down across from Elizabeth. "Do you not think the ride to London a perfect length for conversation? You and Georgiana should ride with us. We can put our luggage in the extra carriage and have plenty of room for our entire party."

Darcy finally looked up. "I shall ride my stallion tomorrow," he said. "While I would normally entreat you to entertain Georgiana for the ride, it shall not be necessary tomorrow. Miss Elizabeth travels to London with us, and will be company for Georgiana." He turned back to the row of books.

"Miss Elizabeth travels—" Caroline stopped, once again visibly surprised.

Elizabeth took advantage of the few moments of silence that followed while Caroline processed all the implications of Mr. Darcy's statement.

"Mr. Darcy, I fear I must also interrupt your perusal to remind you of my need for writing supplies." Perhaps it would have been more proper to ask Miss Bingley, but Elizabeth suddenly felt drained from the events of the morning. Rude as Mr. Darcy was, he at least did not pretend to be her friend. Engaging in a conversation with Miss Bingley would take far more energy than Elizabeth cared to exert at the moment.

"Of course," he replied. "Miss Bingley, I am certain you would not mind loaning Miss Elizabeth your writing set for a short time, would you? She only needs to write a short letter."

Miss Bingley agreed that she would not in a manner that communicated to Elizabeth just how much she did mind.

"I must ask yet a greater favor," Elizabeth said as she collected the supplies and sat back down to write, "for I have two letters to write rather than one, though both shall be short."

"Two?" Mr. Darcy asked, turning from the book he had finally selected.

"Yes, I must send a note to my aunt and uncle as well as to Jane."

Understanding the situation, Darcy nodded once and returned to his book. Caroline pounced on the chance. "Is this your aunt and uncle in Cheapside? Certainly you do not go to Town to see them, I must presume," she added, lifting her head slightly as if daring Elizabeth to contradict her.

Elizabeth smiled, refusing to take the bait. "Why, yes, of course. I do so look forward to seeing how much my cousins have grown since my last visit." She bent her head over her letters. Twenty-four hours, and she could be talking with her Aunt Madeline in the Gardiners' sunny drawing room on Gracechurch Street. No more Darcy, no

28

more Caroline Bingley. Twenty-four hours couldn't be that hard, surely. Quickly composing and sealing her letters, Elizabeth handed them off to a servant and looked back to where Georgiana still sat at the chess board.

"Do you play chess, Miss Georgiana?" she asked.

Across the room, Mr. Darcy looked up quickly, but did not say anything. Elizabeth refused to turn his way, even though she could feel his eyes on her.

"A little," Georgiana said. "William taught me last winter."

Elizabeth smiled. Chess would be a perfect distraction from the companions who didn't want her there, and hopefully would shield Georgiana from being petted and talked at by Caroline. "Lovely."

CHAPTER FOUR

Having had ample time to observe Caroline Bingley's tenacity where Mr. Darcy was involved, Elizabeth had braced herself to spend the day enduring Caroline's condescension, likely made more pronounced by her exaggerated flattery of Georgiana. Her expectations did not take into account that Mr. Darcy, having traveled with the Bingleys several times before, had planned so this very situation could be avoided.

It did not surprise Elizabeth to find Mr. Darcy in the breakfast room when she came down the next morning. During her time at Netherfield when Jane was ill, she had faced several awkward mornings alone with him and an equally silent servant before the others awoke and joined them. The fact that he looked up and smiled when she came in, however, caught her completely off guard.

"Good, you're up. I hope to get an early start on our journey. Can you be ready to leave in half an hour?"

"But what about Miss Georgiana?" Elizabeth replied.

"My sister is awake and will be down shortly."

"Well then yes, I can be."

"Good." He went back to drinking his coffee.

Elizabeth made her selections from the sideboard and sat down several places from Mr. Darcy. To her surprise, he looked up again and studied her. "You are wearing the same dress as yesterday."

She flushed. "I am, sir. I would not have felt right taking another of Miss Darcy's dresses from her, and despite what you must think, I *am* occasionally capable of wearing a dress for several hours without ruining it."

Several seconds passed in silence, then he said, "It suits you."

Elizabeth's head snapped up and she stared at him, certain she had misheard. Mr. Darcy, give a genuine compliment to *her*? Impossible.

"Well, then," she finally managed, "it is a good thing that Miss Darcy does not care for stripes."

He frowned slightly, still studying her—likely it hadn't occurred to him that his sister had preferences, Elizabeth thought spitefully—and at that moment footsteps sounded outside the door. They both flinched and looked away and when Georgiana entered the room moments later it was to find two people utterly absorbed with their breakfast.

To Elizabeth's surprise, Georgiana immediately went to her brother and kissed his cheek. "Good morning William, Miss Elizabeth," she said brightly. "Is it not a wonderful day?"

"I see I do not need to ask how you are this morning," Mr. Darcy remarked, but he put a hand on Georgiana's arm and raised his eyebrows at her nonetheless.

Her smile dimmed slightly. "I am well," she said quietly. "Better. I am glad we leave for Town today."

"You had best eat something before we leave," Elizabeth said lightly. "I fear Mr. Darcy will leave us both to make our own way to London if we do not hurry."

"He wouldn't!" Georgiana exclaimed. "Besides, he will not be taking the carriage."

"No, but we must stop at Longbourn to collect Miss Elizabeth's things, and I should like to be there when we do."

"You needn't worry yourself," Elizabeth said. "I doubt most of the household will be up yet, and there is no cause for ceremony." Even as she spoke, though, she felt a twinge of anxiety at her reception. Would Mr. Collins be there? Could he have convinced her father that they must be married?

"Certainly even your father would not like his daughter traveling to town with near strangers and no say in the matter," Mr. Darcy said coldly.

Elizabeth blanched, and Georgiana looked up at her brother in surprise.

"Besides," Mr. Darcy went on in a somewhat less bitter tone, "your distress over Mr. Collins yesterday was considerable. Should he attempt anything, ah, *unpleasant*, I daresay he would listen to me more than you or your father."

"You *are* the great Lady Catherine de Bourgh's nephew," Elizabeth said archly. "And I must say you are correct—he has proven that he will not listen to me at all." She looked up and met his gaze steadily. "I do not make a practice of running from men simply because they are unfavorable or ridiculous."

Darcy's eyebrows snapped together. "He did not hurt you, did he?" he asked, voice tight.

Elizabeth dropped her eyes. "He did not, sir. Although I must say I left before he worked through the fact that I was indeed rejecting him. If I am lucky, he will have realized by now that me running away was not simply another way to *increase his love by suspense*." She bit out the last few words, fist clenching around the spoon she had been using to stir sugar into her tea.

Looking up, Elizabeth found Georgiana wide-eyed with surprise and concern, and Darcy's face unreadable. Her temper ebbed as quickly as it had risen, and she said simply, "Forgive me." Certainly Georgiana could understand the frustration of unwanted advances, and Mr. Darcy was free to think what he liked.

They quitted the breakfast room soon after. Elizabeth, with no other possessions, went directly to the waiting carriage and stood admiring how the sunrise colored the landscape while she waited for the Darcys.

Mr. Darcy emerged before his sister, his valet and a servant who carried his trunk close behind. Passing Elizabeth to mount his waiting horse, he paused. "Is there any reason to fear your father might insist upon your acceptance of Mr. Collins?" he asked quietly, reaching out to adjust one of the carriage horse's bridle as though his stopping required an excuse.

"I do not believe so, sir," she replied in a tone as low as his own. "My father would not force me to do something so against my wishes."

"Even for the good of your family?"

They had avoided any eye contact thus far, but at this Elizabeth turned and looked up at him. "We shall see soon," she said frankly. Marrying Mr. Collins meant the end of her family's financial worries—but how could she live with the man? Let alone... The thought of conjugal relations made her drop her gaze to the ground abruptly, cheeks heating.

"Elizabeth?"

His over-familiarity shocked her, but she kept her eyes firmly on the hem of Georgiana's dress. "Yes, Mr. Darcy?"

There was a long pause, as if he did not know how to proceed. Finally, he said, "I have not seen Georgiana so happy with a companion in some time."

"Miss Bingley's flattery does not suit her?" she asked without thinking. Brain catching up to her mouth, she gave a short gasp. What was it about this dratted man that made her unable to hold her tongue!

"Miss Bingley wants for authenticity," he said, surprising her. Well, he already knew she was opinionated and outspoken, Elizabeth reasoned. If her words still shocked him, she would have to consider him slow.

"I shall add that to your list of characteristics a female must possess," she said, forcing herself to look up and praying that the flush she felt on her cheeks was not too pronounced.

He was looking directly at her. "You have sisters, Miss Elizabeth. Surely you understand I would do a great deal to ensure my sister's happiness. Would you not do the same?"

Yes, she thought. He would talk to someone below his rank whom he found simply tolerable because his sister liked the person. Aloud, she said,

"Perhaps not for *all* of my sisters, Mr. Darcy. Some of them could do with a bit more seriousness in their lives. But do not fear I misunderstand you. There is nothing in this world that would keep me from doing all that I could for Jane." Thinking of Mr. Bingley and Jane's certain disappointment, Elizabeth turned on her heel and walked away. Not waiting for someone to hand her into the carriage, she climbed in and let the door close, leaving Mr. Darcy staring after her.

CHAPTER FIVE

As Elizabeth had predicted, Longbourn was quiet when they pulled up outside. Kitty, Lydia, and Mrs. Bennet were not awake to come to the window of the drawing room as they usually did when visitors arrived. The welcoming committee consisted of Jane and Mr. Bennet, the former of who looked anxious while the latter looked stern. Elizabeth's trunk sat beside them, though, which reassured her somewhat.

Again, Elizabeth did not wait for assistance to exit the carriage. She jumped down and went directly to her father, eyes asking the question she could not say aloud.

"Well, Lizzy," he started sternly, looking down at her, "you've put the household in quite an uproar. But then I suppose it is not your way to do things predictably. Traveling with a man I know you despise, for instance," his eyes flicked to Mr. Darcy, who was dismounting several yards away, "well, I would not have expected it of you."

"Lizzy, your hand," Jane exclaimed, breaking in. "Your dress! Whatever happened to you?"

"I fell," Elizabeth said, sticking to the story she had decided upon the day before. "I cut my hand and ruined my dress. I had happened to meet Miss Darcy not long before, and she insisted I return to Netherfield with her." It was the same story she had relayed to Jane in her note, which her father had likely read by now.

"How lucky it is," Mr. Bennet remarked, "that Netherfield should be there to house my daughters when they find themselves in less than perfect health."

Elizabeth glanced back to see Mr. Darcy handing Georgiana down from the carriage, no doubt close enough to have heard Mr. Bennet. Ignoring her father—and her surprise that Mr. Darcy found her family worthy of meeting his sister—she smiled at Georgiana and made the introductions. Georgiana responded to the greetings timidly, then fell silent and moved so she stood partially behind Elizabeth.

With no more delays available, Elizabeth took a deep breath and faced her sister. "How fares my mother?" she asked.

Jane looked distressed at having to bear news she knew Elizabeth would not like. Both girls glanced at their father, but he remained silent. "My mother has taken to her bed," Jane said when it was clear Mr. Bennet did not plan to speak. She is most distressed and I fear blames you."

It was the answer Elizabeth had expected, and she nodded once, realizing a moment later through her distraction that she had copied Mr. Darcy's typical response. "And my father?" she asked. This was the answer she could not anticipate, and she could not quite keep the tremor from her voice as the question was asked.

Mr. Bennet was now forced to speak. "Well, Lizzy," he said slowly, "as entertaining as it would have been to have such a fool for a son-in-law, I cannot sentence you to any man from whom you feel you must run."

A wave of relief crashed over Elizabeth, and she felt herself sag slightly. "Thank you, Papa," she said with feeling.

"And will you still be leaving us for London?" Mr. Bennet asked. "Or was that simply to be your escape should I insist that you marry Mr. Collins?"

"Papa!" Elizabeth and Jane exclaimed together, sharing a quick look.

"Mr. Collins was noticeably irritable and sullen when I saw him last; perhaps it is still better that you go."

"I should like to go to my aunt and uncle Gardiner," Elizabeth continued, forcing herself to remain calm. "Miss Darcy kindly offered me passage with her, and I saw no reason why I ought not accept. I can return with my aunt and uncle when they come for the Christmas holidays in a month." It was a very direct statement and would have offered offence with many of the men of Elizabeth's acquaintance—Mr. Darcy was certainly one! —but her father had always hated women who hinted rather than declared their intentions and desires.

"Very well then, Lizzy. I shall see you on your return, though I already mourn the loss of your conversation in the meantime. There will be far too much talk of nothing but ribbons and beaux without you here."

At the mention of beaux, he raised an eyebrow slightly. Alarm bells went off in Lizzy's head. Surely he could not mean to bring up Mr. Wickham, and yet she knew her father too well to think him incapable of such a comment. Had it not been for Wickham's involvement with the Darcy family, any remark may have actually been more appropriate than what Mr. Bennet had said so far. From the shift at her side, she knew that Mr. Darcy had perceived the same pending trouble. After all, she had told him quite plainly two nights ago that she far preferred Mr. Wickham to him. Such stupid, stupid words!

"You do my sister and I a great favor by allowing her Miss Elizabeth's company for the journey, sir," Mr. Darcy cut in smoothly. "I shall ensure that she reaches her relatives safely, and I am sure Miss Elizabeth will not object to writing you upon her arrival."

Mr. Bennet waved him off, but Elizabeth could see the appraisal in his eyes. "She may write to Jane," he said, "and then Jane can tell us far happier news than we actually received, with all the characters painted in a light they have not earned." He turned to go, giving Elizabeth a final nod and smile in good-bye.

Elizabeth stepped forward to embrace Jane, and in the commotion of loading her trunk onto the carriage next to Miss Darcy's much newer one, found the chance to whisper, "Do not worry, Jane, I am fine. But—do not trust Mr. Wickham. We have been deceived about his character."

Jane's eyes widened in alarm, but Mr. Darcy stood waiting to hand Elizabeth into the carriage, and there was no time to say more. "I will write, I promise," Elizabeth said. "Good-bye, dearest Jane."

With a final smile, she turned and accepted Mr. Darcy's hand. They had not touched since the Netherfield ball, and she found herself overly aware of the heat that came through his glove. And was it her imagination, or had he gripped her hand rather tighter than necessary?

"Mr. Darcy," Mr. Bennet called. Both Darcy and Elizabeth flinched. Mr. Darcy finished handing her in, then closed the carriage door on her and Georgiana and turned to face her father. Though she could see them perfectly through the carriage window, Mr. Bennet spoke too quietly for her to make out his words. Mr. Darcy replied at the same volume, and neither man's countenance gave away

41

enough for Elizabeth to guess their words. Then Mr. Darcy gave his signature nod, doffed his hat and bowed slightly to Jane, and re-mounted his horse.

Elizabeth breathed a sigh of relief as the carriage began to move. As stressful as the meeting had been, dealing with Mrs. Bennet or Mr. Collins would have been far worse. She waved once more to Jane, then settled herself on the seat.

"I like your sister," Georgiana said brightly as they turned onto the road, her shyness completely gone. "She is kind, and very beautiful."

Elizabeth laughed. "That she is. Do you know, I once decided to hate her for being so much prettier than me, but I couldn't do it. Jane is genuinely good, and she never once has flaunted her beauty."

"But you are beautiful!" Georgiana exclaimed.

"I am tolerable, perhaps," Elizabeth replied, wishing Darcy was there to hear the exchange. How she would love to see him squirm! "You would not think me beautiful if I stood next to Jane, as I so often do. Do not be concerned," she added, seeing Georgiana's concerned expression. "I am happy enough with my looks, and I daresay I would misuse great beauty if I had it." She stuck her nose in the air and looked around the carriage with exaggerated disdain.

Georgiana giggled, completely different than the painfully shy girl that Elizabeth had seen with everyone besides herself and Mr. Darcy. Mr. Darcy, Elizabeth could understand—they were siblings, even if the man was stuffy and tended towards rudeness. But herself, how to explain that? Could it really been as simple as coming to Georgiana's rescue the day before and not blaming her for the situation?

Unaware of Elizabeth's thoughts, Georgiana beamed. "It is so pleasant to have a traveling companion with whom to talk. Mrs. Annesley usually travels with me, but she falls asleep the second the carriage starts moving."

"Does Mr. Darcy always ride?" Elizabeth asked.

"No, not always," Georgiana said. She frowned. "I have not traveled with him very often lately, or I should say, not *just* him. He will ride in the carriage if it is just the two of us and my companion. I used to love nothing better than traveling with William, because he always reads to me, and he is such a delightful reader. It is when there are others in our party that he rides his horse."

"Does he not like large companies?" Elizabeth tried to wrap her head around the idea of Mr. Darcy reading to entertain his much younger sister in a bumpy coach with difficulty. To instruct, perhaps, but surely he did not read to entertain.

"No," Georgiana said again, but stopped. "He, that is, I believe he, well, I don't really know."

"Do not feel that you have to tell me anything you do not feel comfortable with," Elizabeth said, watching Georgiana struggle with her thoughts.

"It is not that, I like talking to you, I am only unsure if I am correct. I have not been with William for several of his most recent journeys, but it occurred to me that he rides separately if there are unmarried ladies—other than myself, of course—in the party. I do not mean to say he avoids ladies in general, or means anything by it, but—" she stopped abruptly.

"But when he is around unmarried women, they are either intimidated by him and say nothing, or throw themselves at him in an attempt to become the next Mrs. Darcy," Elizabeth finished for her.

"Exactly! That is why I was so excited to speak with you, or at least partly why. You clearly knew who he was, but did not shy away or flatter him."

Because I dislike him, Elizabeth thought wryly, *and I suppose I have already proven without a doubt that I will not marry a man I do not like for a position I can live without.*

Georgiana went on, "That is why I decided to trust you. That, and you were so genuinely kind to me after, well, after."

"I am honored to be your friend," Elizabeth said, smiling. "I hope we shall have many experiences together, all much happier than the circumstances in which we met."

"Oh, me too," Georgiana said. "Me too. Tell me, do you play piano?"

*

They reached Gracechurch Street that afternoon. Georgiana exclaimed over the picturesqueness of the Gardiners' brick house with its brightly painted shutters and flowerpots framing the front door. Elizabeth answered her comments and questions rather absently, far more interested to see the inhabitants than the house itself.

"Do you have many cousins?" Georgiana asked as the carriage came to a stop and several small faces appeared in an upstairs window.

"Yes, four," Elizabeth replied. "Two girls and two boys. Thomas, Julia, Eleanor, and William. I must admit I am a horrible cousin for saying this, but William is my favorite. He is—" she broke off, for Mr. Darcy had opened the door and was staring at her. She stared back for several long seconds, unsure of what to say and all too aware that "William" was what Georgiana called him.

"Miss Elizabeth has been telling me about her cousins," Georgina said, coming to the rescue. "Thomas, Julia, Eleanor, and William, am I right,

Lizzy? I do wish I had younger cousins. It would be so fun to have children to play with."

Elizabeth forced herself to look away from Mr. Darcy. "I am certain my cousins would be happy to play with you, Georgiana," she said as lightly as she could manage. "When they wear me out I shall send for you to take a turn."

"That sounds wonderful," Georgiana said, taking her brother's hand and stepping down from the carriage.

He turned back to offer his hand to Elizabeth, who accepted it gingerly and snatched her hand back as soon as her feet touched the ground. "You need not stay," she said quietly, so that Georgiana could not hear her. "I am sure you must be anxious to reach your home."

"You are mistaken, Miss Elizabeth," he replied. "I should like to meet your aunt and uncle, and I am certain Georgiana does as well."

Elizabeth raised her eyebrows and glanced over at Georgiana. Miss Darcy, happy to meet new people? Looking back at Mr. Darcy, she saw he understood. "It will be good for her to meet more people, and those not in her immediate circle," he added.

Ah, yes, Elizabeth thought, *let the princess meet the paupers.* But the sentiment did not ring true. For one thing, the princess stood looking around herself with an air of delight, taking in the bustle of Gracechurch Street. For another—

The front door burst open and three-year-old William ran out, Julia on his heels. "William, no!" she cried. "Mama said you must wait!"

"Lis-beth!" William said, ignoring his older sister. He stopped suddenly, looking up at her shyly, then glancing at Georgiana and back. "Lis-beth?"

"Dearest," Elizabeth said, bending to scoop up her youngest cousin and running her nose through his curls to make him laugh. "I have missed you!"

"Lis-beth," he said happily, tucking his head down on her shoulder and sticking his tongue out at Julia.

"William," Elizabeth admonished. "That was *not* a gentlemanly thing to do."

The door opened again and Mrs. Gardiner came out, eyes widening as she took in Elizabeth's companions. "Lizzy, it is so good to see you. It appears that some of us were too excited to wait a moment longer for your arrival. You are all that William has talked about since we received your letter. Please, come in, all of you, and we can have our proper introductions indoors."

CHAPTER SIX

Mrs. Gardiner led the way to the drawing room. Once there, Mr. Darcy stood awkwardly and Georgiana linked her hands tightly together in front of her. Elizabeth, recognizing her stance, realized that shyness had struck Georgiana again. She stepped forward and made the necessary introductions, including all of her cousins. Georgiana seemed to lose some of the tension in her shoulders as she greeted the younger Gardiners, although her voice barely raised above a whisper.

Mrs. Gardiner shooed the children back out of the room into the care of a waiting maid. "You can see Cousin Elizabeth soon," she said firmly. Elizabeth brought William over and handed him to the maid, adding her own promise to come visit them in the nursery once the Darcys had left.

"Are you by chance the Pemberley Darcys?" Mrs. Gardiner asked when the children were gone and they had all seated themselves.

Mr. Darcy's slight frown grew more pronounced at the question. Elizabeth opened her mouth to snap that her aunt didn't care how much money he had a year, and wouldn't ask even if she did care.

Mrs. Gardiner did not need defense, however. She went on, "I grew up in Lambton, not five miles from Pemberley, and I am always eager for news of that area. When we travel it is usually to

Hertfordshire," she inclined her head towards Elizabeth, "and I have not been home in some ten years. Derbyshire is a lovely area, and I miss it greatly some days."

Darcy's frown turned to a look of interest. "Indeed, madam, I feel your pain. I have not been home for more than several months these last few years. We have a fine house in Town, of course, but it lacks some of the qualities I prize most about Pemberley."

"Mr. Darcy, a fan of country life?" Elizabeth could not help teasing. "I must confess my surprise. Miss Bingley painted you as a most ardent admirer of London."

"In some regards, I am," he returned seriously. "One cannot hope to match London's command of the arts, its varied entertainment, nor its capacity to conduct trade, no matter how much effort is put into the attempt when in the country. It also provides a far greater social scene."

"I'll have you know we dine with four-and-twenty families in Hertfordshire," Elizabeth said, turning up her nose in an exaggerated fashion.

Mr. Darcy looked taken aback, then gave a small smile as he recognized her words for a jab at her mother. "Surely *you* cannot have always been in Hertfordshire," he said.

It was Elizabeth's turn to sit back in surprise, blinking as she tried to understand his meaning.

"Elizabeth and Jane visit us for at least a fortnight each year," Mrs. Gardiner said, smoothly covering Elizabeth's confusion. "We would keep them longer, but you are not the only one fond of the country, Mr. Darcy." She turned to Georgiana, who had been silent since the younger Gardiners left. "Which do you prefer, Miss Darcy?"

Georgiana looked at her brother, then Elizabeth. Finally, she glanced up shyly at Mrs. Gardiner. "I like both," she said, looking away again. "I, uh, I miss Derbyshire as well. I should like to spend more time there."

"Does Mr. Thomason still have a sweet shop in Lambton?" Mrs. Gardiner asked her.

"Yes," Georgiana said in a voice barely above a whisper.

"I used to get the most wonderful marzipan from Mr. Thomason," Mrs. Gardiner said. "Have you ever tried it? I have yet to find a sweet store in London that can boast true superiority over Mr. Thomason's marzipan."

Georgiana gave an honest, full smile. "William—Mr. Darcy—used to bring me marzipan from Mr. Thomason. I have not had any in some time, though."

"You must have a piece for me when you go next. I would insist you have a piece for Miss Elizabeth, too, but I fear she would tell you to not eat it."

"Whyever not?" Georgiana asked, just as Darcy said, "You do not like marzipan, Miss Elizabeth?"

Elizabeth laughed at their concern over sweets. "My aunt does me a disservice. She has the distinct advantage of knowing me as a child, when each new experience evoked a far stronger emotion than it does at the present time. The first marzipan I saw was in the shape of a beautiful swan. Kitty—my younger sister Catherine," she added for Georgiana's sake "—was only two or three years old at the time. She grabbed two fistfuls of the marzipan and shoved them both in her mouth. I was so angry with her for ruining the swan, I couldn't eat marzipan on principle for years."

Elizabeth had been focused on Georgiana, excited to see her look up from her lap, but she glanced towards Mr. Darcy as she finished her story. Expecting to see disdain at her sister's lack of decorum, his smile caught her off guard. She smiled back hesitantly.

"We have the most wonderful marzipan sculptures at Christmas," Georgiana said, laughing at Elizabeth's story. "You would certainly find them hard to eat!"

Mr. Darcy's smile vanished. "Georgiana, I fear we must go if we are to be settled in time for supper," he said abruptly.

Georgiana looked at him in surprise, then collected herself and rose readily. Elizabeth marveled at her composure—*she* would have made an impertinent comment in response to his overbearing tone. *How awful for Georgiana, to be so accustomed to such comments that they were followed without thought or resistance!* Elizabeth thought. *I should never be able to live with such a man.*

The rest of the party rose as well, and farewells were said. Georgiana hinted at Elizabeth's coming to visit at Darcy House twice and even managed a full smile at Mrs. Gardiner. Darcy was nearly silent, speaking only as much as required by social convention. Just before he quit the room, however, he turned back and looked at Elizabeth. "I hope you find your time in Town enjoyable, Miss Elizabeth, despite your preference for the country."

She curtsied, completely unsure of his meaning and therefore how to respond. Then the Darcys were gone and Elizabeth was left alone with her aunt.

"Well, Lizzy," Mrs. Gardiner said, "you shall have to tell me how you came to be traveling in such company, and with so little notice! We received your letter not two hours before you arrived yourself. I have never found you given to rash decisions on a large scale, and must confess myself concerned at the cause of your arrival. And is not Mr. Darcy the very man you described in great disdain in your last letter?"

Elizabeth stifled a sigh. There was no use keeping secrets from her aunt. In many ways, Mrs. Gardiner was a better confidant than even Jane, for she lent far more experience to her observations. "He is, although I have since had reason to doubt the credibility of my primary source of information, if not my own observations. He is without doubt a proud, arrogant man, but his faults beyond that I cannot say."

"I daresay a man of Mr. Darcy's standing has a right to be proud," Mrs. Gardiner said. "And as for arrogant, I saw someone perhaps ill at ease in his situation today, but no arrogance. I imagine he must be wary of conversing with young ladies and their families, for a great number must think only of securing a favorable marriage." She lifted one eyebrow at her niece.

Elizabeth flushed slightly, which vexed her, for marriage to Mr. Darcy was the last thing she desired, and she told her aunt as much. "Were it not for Miss Georgiana, I should be happy to never see him again," she went on, "but she is a sweet girl and I believe does not have many friends—perhaps because, as you say, most young ladies are interested in the brother and use the sister only as a means of reaching him. Miss Caroline Bingley, for example, could not praise Georgiana enough when it kept Mr. Darcy's attention on her, and yet had nothing to say to Georgiana herself."

"It is plain that Mr. Darcy cares a great deal for his sister, but I believe your liveliness will do her good. She was quite young when both her parents died—ten years old, or thereabouts. She has lived with a governess or companion since then, and her brother is old enough to be more of a father than a playmate."

"You know a great deal about the Darcys," Elizabeth exclaimed. "I never would have suspected!"

"The Darcys were the great landowners where I grew up," Mrs. Gardiner said. "We all kept track of their doings. I left not long before this Mr. Darcy inherited Pemberley, but his father was a kind and generous man. I was sad to hear of his passing."

Elizabeth opened her mouth to say that yes, the father had been both of those while the son was neither, and then snapped it shut again as she recalled the source of her information. How long would it take her to work out the lies that Mr. Wickham had told, especially since she wasn't sure which of his statements were fabricated and which had their roots in fact?

Fortunately, Mrs. Gardiner did not seem inclined to press her niece on her behavior, turning instead to the reason for Elizabeth's visit to Town. Relieved to find a sympathetic ear, Elizabeth recounted the events of the previous day, omitting only the details of how she had met Georgiana.

"Well, Lizzy dear," Mrs. Gardiner said once she had finished, "that was perhaps a more impulsive act than I would have expected from you. But it is done now and I can't say I am unhappy to have you here. If anyone asks we need only say it was a planned visit so you could visit with your cousins and purchase your Christmas presents here in Town. I must admit, I will be grateful of your help with the children. William gets into everything, and Julia has started refusing to do anything with Eleanor of late."

"I shall be delighted to spend time with my cousins," Elizabeth responded. "And as for Christmas shopping, perhaps Julia could go with me. I remember feeling very grown up at her age and hating to be classified as a child with Mary and Kitty. It may help her be kinder to Eleanor if she is treated more like a young lady, if only for a few hours."

"That is a delightful idea," Mrs. Gardiner said. "Let's wait to tell her, though, or she will want to go this very instant. Perhaps tomorrow, after you have returned Miss Darcy's visit, or the day after. I get the feeling that Miss Darcy will be just as disappointed as Julia if you do not go to Darcy House tomorrow, and she has the advantage of knowing the plan already."

Laughing, Elizabeth stood. "You are probably right, as usual. Now, I daresay my cousins will come bursting in here soon if I do not go find them." Mrs. Gardiner agreed, and they left the room together.

As she climbed the stairs towards the nursery, Elizabeth could not help but wonder at the feelings that the mention of visiting Georgiana had evoked. She looked forward to calling on her new friend, and the thought of Georgiana's honest excitement over the visit made her happy. But Darcy himself— did she wish to see him, so she could form a better understanding of what the man was like in his own world? Or did she hope to avoid him, for certainly the wolf would be protective of his den and likely twice as proud and high-handed as normal?

They reached the nursery door before Elizabeth realized it, lost as she was in her thoughts. And when her cousins immediately demanded her full attention, leaving her with no room for such thoughts, she could not say that she minded the distraction.

CHAPTER SEVEN

When the carriage pulled up to Darcy House the next day, Elizabeth sat and stared for a moment. To know that Mr. Darcy had ten thousand a year was one thing. Knowing he owned a townhouse on Grosvenor Street was similar—impressive, but not overwhelming.

Seeing it was different. The house was massive and intimidating, the street seemingly empty after the bustle of Gracechurch Street. Elizabeth had no trouble imagining that many of the merchants and tradesmen who lived near her aunt and uncle had never set foot in Grosvenor Street and likely never would. The whole area gave off an air that said all too clearly, *Only people of fashion may pass here.* Despite her usual disregard for such restrictions, Elizabeth might have ordered the driver to return her home at once, had Georgiana's pale face not appeared in a first-story window.

Elizabeth steeled herself. Miss Darcy had to *live* here. Surely she, Elizabeth, could stand a half-hour's visit. She exited the carriage, walked up the wide steps to the front door, and knocked before she could stop herself.

The door opened almost immediately, revealing a liveried footman. Presenting her card—thank goodness Jane had thought to pack them for her—she asked for Miss Darcy.

The footman surveyed her critically, reminding Elizabeth keenly that her dress was hardly up to Town standards, but took the card and motioned her into the entryway. "I shall enquire if Miss Darcy is home," he said. "I believe she may have gone out this morning. Wait here, please."

Yes, I know you don't think I'm good enough to call here, Elizabeth thought to herself, watching his back retreat up the stairs. What she would give to be a fly on the wall when Georgiana told the footman to show her up!

Focused on the stairs in the hopes that some of the footman's shock would still be on his face, Elizabeth missed the door opening not twenty feet from her. "Miss Elizabeth," Darcy said, closing the door behind him and coming towards her. "I had not thought to see you again so soon."

Thought, or hoped? Elizabeth wondered, wishing she dared to ask aloud. She managed a polite smile. "I have come to return Miss Darcy's visit. The kindness shown in visiting my aunt and myself yesterday when you must have wished to reach home did not go unnoticed. I did not wish yourself or Miss Georgiana to think me backwards in my attentions."

"The pleasure was all ours," Mr. Darcy responded. "Your aunt is a charming lady."

Now the footman returned, and Elizabeth had the pleasure of seeing his jaw drop as he took in the scene in the entryway. "Mr. Darcy!" he stuttered. "I thought you and Miss Darcy were out today, sir."

Mr. Darcy's mouth twitched, and Elizabeth wondered if the footman had been instructed to say just that, should anyone come to call. "I have returned only recently, Harris," he said calmly.

Harris was too well trained to gape, but Elizabeth could see the footman struggle to catch up with the situation. He turned to Elizabeth and gave a slight bow. "Miss Darcy is, ah, also at home. Shall I show you to the drawing room?"

"Do not bother, Harris, I shall show her myself," Mr. Darcy said, startling another wide-eyed look out of him. He turned to Elizabeth. "This way, Miss Elizabeth."

Elizabeth began to feel for Harris, whose world had clearly been turned on its ear by her appearance and warm welcome. She gave him a sincere smile, which seemed to shock him even more, and followed Mr. Darcy up the stairs.

"I believe I have frightened your footman, coming in all my heathen apparel," Elizabeth said quietly as they climbed.

Mr. Darcy glanced back and gave her an inscrutable look. "Harris is new; he is not accustomed to hiding his thoughts as he should."

"I found it endearing," Elizabeth retorted.

Darcy stopped abruptly, and Elizabeth stumbled as she tried to avoid colliding with him. He turned quickly and caught her by her shoulders. For a second neither party moved. Standing one step lower than he, Elizabeth found herself staring at Mr. Darcy's chest. She looked up, past his elaborately tied cravat, and found him gazing down at her. His eyes were not black as she had thought, but a dark brown with lighter flecks mixed in. She blinked.

"Must you always look down at me, Mr. Darcy?" Elizabeth asked, stepping out of his grasp carefully and moving sideways. Heaven help her if she took a tumble down the stairs!

Mr. Darcy stared at her a moment longer. "Our respective heights make that a rather incurable problem, Miss Elizabeth. Or should you wish that I sit down every time you address me, so that you may have the privilege of looking down at me?"

"I suppose it is a situation to which I must resign myself," she responded archly, stepping up one stair so the difference was less pronounced. "After all, to have one's every wish fulfilled is harmful for one's character." *And you see, Mr. Darcy, I do not wish to be like you.*

"It most certainly does not always help one's situation in life," Mr. Darcy said tightly, his stare hardening for a moment before he broke eye contact and continued up the stairs. Left gaping, Elizabeth stumbled again as she hurried to follow him. This time, he did not even look back.

She followed him up the rest of the stairs and halfway down a wide hallway. He halted and turned back. "Thank you for visiting my sister," he said in a voice that belonged to a different man than the one on the stairs moments ago. "She was very hopeful that you would call today."

"Of course," Elizabeth responded, confused and rather cross because of it. Was he determined to thwart every attempt to understand him? "Miss Darcy is delightful company."

He gave a brief but seemingly genuine smile, then opened the door and bowed her through it. "Miss Elizabeth is here to see you, Georgiana."

Georgiana exclaimed from across the room and rose to greet her guest, but Elizabeth found herself watching Darcy, wondering what he would do next. He gave her a curt nod, expression unreadable, and closed the door between them, leaving her alone with Georgiana.

Elizabeth collected herself and turned to greet Georgiana properly. "I fear I have distressed both Mr. Darcy and your footman with my visit," Elizabeth said teasingly once the original pleasantries had been exchanged.

To her surprise, Georgiana laughed outright. "Oh, that is all my brother's fault. He did not wish to—" she broke off. "Oh, drat. I oughtn't have said that. William and Mrs. Annesley both tell me that some truths are better left unsaid."

"It is hard being a young lady, is it not?" Elizabeth commiserated. "You must always be gentle and quiet, but make sure not to speak too little, or too much about any one subject. You must discuss everything as though it is pleasant, even if you detest the subject or the person to whom you are speaking. You must," she stopped, wrinkling her nose at Georgiana. "I shall stop there. I have had several reasons of late to reflect on why I dislike being a young lady, but complaining has yet to do me any good."

"But that is exactly what I was thinking!" Georgiana exclaimed. "Mrs. Annesley says that it will become easier, but I have yet to see proof that I will ever be less shy or awkward."

"You are not shy or awkward talking to me," Elizabeth said.

"Oh, but you are different, though," Miss Darcy replied. "You are, well, *easy* to talk to. I feel as if I can speak what is truly on my mind and you will not judge me for it, or tell me that young ladies oughtn't think so."

"Ah, so I am a terrible influence," Elizabeth teased. "I am surprised your brother allows our continued acquaintance."

"No, William likes you," Georgiana said immediately. "He said as much after we left your aunt's house yesterday. And," she stopped and sighed before continuing in a hushed voice, "and I suppose he thinks it will be good for me to have someone to confide in about *him*."

Mr. Darcy, like her? *Certainly not*, Elizabeth thought. But the second part—yes, that she could see. For all his faults, Mr. Darcy cared about his sister. Seeing her unhappy could lead him to see the need for a female confidante, someone she could talk to about her worries. Here was Elizabeth Bennet, a country nobody already acquainted with the Mr. Wickham scandal, but certainly not well enough connected that she could tell anyone who mattered. Were she Mr. Darcy, such an acquaintance may seem desirable. She could be a second companion to Georgiana, until such time as the girl was old and confident enough to make her real, properly dowered and preferably titled friends.

It made perfect sense, but Elizabeth couldn't pretend the thought didn't leave a sour taste in her mouth.

"Do you want to talk about him?" she asked aloud.

"No," Georgiana responded vehemently. "Well, not now, at least. Maybe someday, but now it feels like such a waste of time. Seeing him again at Netherfield made me see that he really isn't worth it. He doesn't matter anymore." Had she not immediately turned away and stared fixedly at her lap, Elizabeth might have believed her. Mr. Wickham himself might mean little now, but the incident had clearly undermined Miss Darcy's confidence in herself. That problem would not be so easily overcome.

"I understand," Elizabeth told her friend. "But please, don't hesitate to bring it up if you need to talk about him. You needn't even make it pleasant for my sake," she added to lighten the tone of the conversation. Then, seeing that Georgiana had no desire to say more, she changed the subject to where she might find the best ribbons and lace to take home to her sisters.

They were still speaking of their favorite places to shop in London—Georgiana's being in a rather different part of town than Elizabeth's—when the door opened again to admit a maid carrying a tray of tea things. She moved slowly across the room and had just placed the tray on a table when the door opened yet again to admit Mr. Darcy. For once, Elizabeth found it easy to ignore him as she focused on the maid. The girl, who couldn't be older than fourteen, was pale and beads of sweat followed her hairline. Dark circles rimmed her eyes, and despite the icy white pallor of the rest of her skin, red circles flared on her cheeks.

Elizabeth knew better than to speak out in front of another person's servant, but she had to grit her teeth to keep from saying something immediately. Georgiana's eyes were once again on her hands, folded in her lap. Darcy appeared to be brooding about something—he had stridden to the window without a word and stood looking down on the street. Distracted, Elizabeth stared at his profile, wondering what on earth could have upset him now.

The sound of shattering china called all of their attention to the center of the room. The maid had been removing a tea cup from her tray when she dropped both cup and saucer onto the floor, where both had shattered. Tea was already seeping into the rug.

Darcy took a step towards the scene with a thunderous look on his face, and Elizabeth reacted without stopping to consider. She stood and placed herself directly between maid and master, facing the latter. His momentum stopped him only a foot from her, and Elizabeth found herself looking directly up at Mr. Darcy for the second time in under half an hour. "She's ill," she hissed, attempting to keep the conversation from reaching the maid. From the sounds behind her, Elizabeth guessed that the girl was fully occupied, but she had learned quickly that just because someone was busy did not mean they were deaf.

"She broke heirloom china and ruined a rug. It is not unreasonable to deliver a scolding."

"By all means, a scolding is in order," Elizabeth said. The angrier she became, the clearer everything seemed. "What in the world was your cook thinking, to send an ill servant to attend your sister, let alone a guest? Is she simple, or just uncaring that sickness spreads? Your maid likely has a fever; she should be in bed! Or are all the servants ill, Mr. Darcy?"

He had stared, open-mouthed, as she berated him. The question seemed to shock him to himself, for his mouth snapped shut. "Do you always interfere in the running of other people's households, Miss Bennet?" Darcy asked acerbically. "Is your country upbringing so superior that you feel a need to overrule policies and standards already in place?"

Elizabeth felt her face flush. "Only when the mistress of the house appears too shy to notice and the master too preoccupied with glaring out of windows to care," she bit out, voice barely above a whisper. "My *country upbringing* has perhaps given me more chance to notice that those who serve me are human as well."

"You go too far, madam," Mr. Darcy said, his face an unreadable mask with cold eyes.

Elizabeth dropped her lowest curtsey in reply. She turned to Georgiana, who had actually bent forward to help the maid collect the last pieces of broken china and appeared to have missed the heat of the exchange. "Miss Darcy, I believe it may be best for me to take this as my signal to leave. I have nearly overstayed my visit anyway, and I do not wish to presume too much. I may be a mere country miss, but I *am* acquainted with the conventions of morning visits."

The last was intended for Mr. Darcy's ears, but he gave no sign that he had heard. Striding across the room, he stopped and turned at the door. "Georgiana, I will be in my study until supper if you need me." Looking at the maid, he went on, "Take that back to the kitchens and send another maid to attend to the rug. You are to go to bed." Finally looking at Elizabeth, he gave her a curt bow that was little more than a jerk of his head. "Good day, Miss Bennet." The door closed and he was gone.

The maid hurried to follow, leaving Georgiana and Elizabeth alone.

"Please forgive William if he has offended you," Georgiana said after several moments of silence. "He is abrupt at times, but he truly means well."

Her anger had not diminished, but Elizabeth's quick mind was already calculating the folly of her words. She had overstepped, that was clear, and it could bring sorrow to the young lady she had begun to truly care for in the past several days. Elizabeth would not make it any harder than she already had.

"If Mr. Darcy is at fault, then I am hardly blameless," she responded quietly, hoping that her angry words had reached Darcy's ears alone. "I am wont to say or do whatever I like and consider the consequences later." She paused, because she did not believe she had been wrong, and would not lie. The words had been ill considered and rashly said, but Elizabeth could not regret defending the maid. "Do not look so worried, dear Georgiana," she continued. "I know my character, and I will not pretend to be something I am not." *There are enough Caroline Bingleys in this world already.*

She glanced over at the younger lady and thought to add a comment so Georgiana would understand that Mr. Darcy's approval truly did not concern her. "That is the main reason I do not plan to every marry. I know that I am not what most men would wish for in a bride, and I can say with certainty that I have yet to meet a man who fulfills what I desire in a husband. Do not look so sad, Georgiana. I am happy how I am."

Georgiana looked concerned, but did not push the matter. "Please do not let William keep you from visiting again," she said.

"If you desire my company, then he could not keep me away," Elizabeth smiled, ignoring the fact that he very well *could* turn her away in the future. "And you are welcome to visit my aunt and uncle's house whenever you wish, for as long as I am in Town. I would be delighted to see you again soon." With that, Elizabeth took her leave, wondering as she exited the house if she would ever see Georgiana again.

CHAPTER EIGHT

Elizabeth spent several quiet but pleasant days in her aunt and cousins' company. She took her cousin Julia shopping for Christmas presents and both had a delightful time. Julia even purchased a ribbon for her younger sister Eleanor without prompting, leading Elizabeth to believe she had been right in assuming Julia simply needed some time away from the younger children. With three younger sisters of her own, Elizabeth understood the need to escape on occasion.

They passed a sweet shop at the end of their shopping, and Julia suggested taking candy back to the others. Elizabeth was happy to comply, although she found herself thinking of her conversation about marzipan with the Darcys for the rest of the walk home. What had Mr. Darcy been thinking when he actually smiled at her that evening? After chasing that train of thought for several minutes, Elizabeth shook her head and admonished herself for not paying attention to Julia's chatter. He certainly had no reason to smile at her now, and that was the end of the matter. Besides, she would return to Longbourn in little over a week, and chances of her seeing either Darcy in Hertfordshire were all but none.

A letter from Jane awaited Elizabeth in the entrance hall, the first she had received since arriving in Town. Hearing the thud of her cousins' footsteps on the stairs, Elizabeth handed the bag of candy to Julia and darted into the haven of her uncle's small library.

Dearest Lizzy,

You must forgive me for not writing sooner, although I am sure you will understand when I tell you all that has happened since you have left. There has been much excitement at Longbourn, and my Mother's nerves have not been well because of it. I fear she holds you somewhat accountable, and so I am glad that you are away with my aunt and uncle and not subjected to her wailings. My Father has retreated to his book room, and the rest of us carry on much as before.

Mr. Collins was quite put out upon discovering your removal to Town, for I daresay he had not given up hope that you should return to Longbourn ready to accept his hand. I never had a chance to tell you, but the evening you were at Netherfield he gave us a great account of the apology he expected and how he should condescend to think of you with even greater favor despite your high spirits and long absence. Dear Lizzy, as much as the rift this proposal has caused distresses me, I am glad you did not accept my cousin. You would have been most unhappy with him.

My cousin, it appears, has not pined for you either. You will scarce believe me, but not two days after you departed for London, he proposed to Miss Lucas and was accepted. He has gone back to Kent to inform Lady Catherine and prepare the parsonage for its mistress. I know not when they are to be wed. Charlotte seems content with the matter, although she did confess to me that she hopes you will not be hurt by the manner in which events took place. Forgive my liberties if they offend you, but I made it known to her that your heart was not involved, even if you pride may be. Dear sister, I hope I have not wronged you, for it did ease Charlotte's mind considerably. Please let me know your mind when you write in return.

I must end here, for my Mother is in need of steadying company, and with Kitty and Lydia gone to Meryton the task has fallen to Mary and myself. Give my love to my aunt and uncle and all my cousins.

Your loving sister,

Jane

Elizabeth sat quietly for several minutes, first staring blankly at the paper and then re-reading sections as she tried to make sense of it all. Charlotte, to marry Mr. Collins! It was impossible! Her friend could not think to tie herself to such a laughingstock of a man. And yet Elizabeth clearly remembered Charlotte's pragmatic views of marriage, as well as her assertion that one could not know too little of a husband's follies before joining him at the altar. Well, she would find innumerable follies in Mr. Collins, Elizabeth had no doubt of that.

The news of her mother's nerves did not concern Lizzy. She had expected no less, and the only emotions she felt were relief in having missed the lion's share of the wailing and regret that Jane had to shoulder the full burden in her absence. Her sister might claim that Mary was helping, but Elizabeth had watched things play out too often to put much stock into such an assertion. Jane would bear the load, assisted only by grave strictures from Mary and flighty comments from Lydia and Kitty as they raced off to find the officers.

Sighing, Elizabeth folded the letter and tucked it into her dress, then made her way to the drawing room in search of a pen and paper. She may not be able to return home to assist Jane at the moment, but at least she could ease her sister's mind by assuring her that no apologies were needed for her words to Charlotte.

The letter was quickly dispatched, including details for her planned return home along with the arrival of the Gardiner's. Lizzy had hoped to ease Jane's mind by letting her know that the present troubles should soon be eased, but the letter that was delivered the next day contained anything but relief.

Lizzy,

I must give you more bad news (though I thank you for your kind reassurances, and hope you know that much happiness has been found through them). Since I wrote last, Mama, Lydia, and Mary have all fallen ill. I have no fever as of yet, but must confess to feeling poorly.

*Please give my regrets to my Aunt
and Uncle, but I beg that you stay in
Town this Christmastime to avoid
any illness. My Father has enclosed
a letter for my Uncle, explaining the
matter farther and giving his
excuses.*

   I hope to hear from you soon.

   Your loving sister,

   Jane

Elizabeth's thoughts went immediately to Mr.
Darcy's ill maid and she flushed as she remembered
the scene. How could she have reprimanded such
an influential man in his own home? Even her
mother, embarrassing and ill-mannered at every
turn, surely would not have done such a thing. And
yet, how could she have done anything differently?
The maid's pale, anxious, and sweat-beaded face
came to mind and Elizabeth couldn't feel regret for
defending the poor girl, even if her own face still
burned with the remembered embarrassment. No,
she was not sorry for her actions, but if she was to
stay in Town through the Christmas season, she
would have to act far more prudently to avoid any
contact with Mr. Darcy.

Sighing, Elizabeth looked back at the letter in her
hand, then down at the missive for her uncle that sat

on her lap. She stood, peeked in her room's small mirror to make sure her face had returned to its normal color, and went to deliver the letter to her uncle—and to tell her aunt that far more decorations would be needed to ready the house for a Christmas spent in Town.

*

The young Gardiners received the news that they were to stay on Gracechurch Street for the holiday with a great deal of excitement and exuberant plans for decorations and schemes. Mrs. Gardiner was far more reserved.

"I'm sorry to keep you from your family for the holiday," she told her niece when at last the children had raced off to begin decorating the nursery. Both women knew that by "family," Mrs. Gardiner really meant "Jane." "I am glad to keep you longer, though, Lizzy, and this way you can hopefully avoid any illness this winter."

"If the illness is not in fact in London," Elizabeth replied without thinking. She had not told her aunt of the scene at the Darcy's house, choosing instead Georgiana's busy schedule as the reason for their lack of contact. That she did not know Georgiana's schedule had been overlooked—Elizabeth could only imagine that Mr. Darcy insist his young sister fill her days with worthwhile activities and accomplishments.

"It is true, there is generally more sickness in Town than the countryside," Mrs. Gardiner said, oblivious to her niece's distraction. "But I hope we shall be healthy enough here." She paused, then continued, "I think it will be a happy Christmas. The children shall like having free reign of decorations, and you must accompany Mr. Gardiner and myself to a Christmas ball or two. I am glad I have not responded to the invitations we received yet—I had not planned to go."

Elizabeth surveyed her aunt's expression carefully. Mrs. Gardiner would never say it, but Elizabeth sensed that she was somewhat relieved at not having to visit her sister-in-law. Fanny Bennet, nee Gardiner, could not be more different than her younger brother's wife. And while Mrs. Gardiner was a welcomed, steadying presence for Mrs. Bennet, the same did not hold true in reverse.

"I don't know about attending balls," Elizabeth said. "I doubt even my best dress would be fine enough for a ball in Town."

"I am sure we can work something out," Mrs. Gardiner replied. "We'll call it your Christmas present, shall we?"

"Aunt, I couldn't accept such a gift!" Lizzy exclaimed.

"Nonsense, of course you could." Mrs. Gardiner brushed off Elizabeth's concern. "Besides, it will be far more amusing for your uncle and I to watch you attract all of the young men. No one pays attention to us old folks anymore. We're just distractions from the splendor of you young ones."

"I believe it's my turn to say 'nonsense,'" Elizabeth retorted. "And I really cannot accept a dress, especially not the kind I would need for a ball!"

The door banged open and Eleanor and Thomas ran in, Julia on their heels with William in her arms. "Lizzy, Lizzy, Lizzy!" Eleanor exclaimed, reaching out to grab Elizabeth's hand and jumping up and down. "Come see, the nursery is so pretty!"

"I hung all of the tall decorations cuz the girls can't climb like me," Thomas said, grabbing her other hand. Together, they tugged her towards the door, all starting to talk over each other. Laughing, Elizabeth dropped a tiny curtsey to her aunt in joking farewell and let herself be pulled upstairs to exclaim over the enthusiastically, if not tastefully, decorated nursery.

*

Christmastime in London was a completely new experience for Lizzy. She had spent several weeks there each winter, often returning with her aunt and uncle after the Christmas festivities, but she had always celebrated the holiday itself at Longbourn. Upon first hearing that she was not to return home as planned, she had thought to be horribly disappointed. As the days passed, however, Elizabeth found herself reveling in the change. She missed Jane dearly and worried for her elder sister, stuck at home with three silly sisters and a sillier mother. Jane's letters painted the picture of a quiet, subdued Longbourn. Lydia had recovered, but Kitty had fallen ill in her place. She, Mary, and Mrs. Bennet continued to be bedridden, although nothing dangerous, Jane was quick to point out. As officers now had no reason to associate with the family—and indeed, to avoid it outright—home was a more peaceful place than it had been when Elizabeth left.

The one sore point in Elizabeth's time in town was the lack of contact from Miss Darcy. Elizabeth had scarcely hoped to hear from Georgiana following the scene with the ill maid, but she discovered that in quiet moments she could not help but wonder how her new friend was faring. What was her Christmas season like, shut up in Darcy House? Was it full of parties and falsely friendly women, or lonely and oppressive with only Mr. Darcy for company?

She got her chance to find out one afternoon, when Julia marched into her room and announced that she could not go another moment in the same house as Eleanor, or else she should have to do something nasty, "And Father says I shan't get any presents if I can't be nice," Julia exclaimed. "But I just *can't* anymore!" She stamped her foot indignantly.

Elizabeth looked up from the letter she was composing to Jane and smothered a smile. How many times had she approached Jane just like this, demanding relief from her own younger sisters? Of course, Jane had been more apt to come up with an activity that all the sisters could enjoy, but Elizabeth could certainly relate with the exasperated, half-desperate expression on her cousin's face.

Making up her mind, she capped her ink bottle and laid down the pen. "How about a walk?" she asked Julia, standing up and shaking out her skirts. "Run and get your pelisse, and we can walk down to Hyde Park."

Julia skipped out, immediately happier. Elizabeth stood up and followed slower, checking the clock in the hall as she collected her own pelisse. *Good. It's still early enough that we will miss the fashionable promenade. Wouldn't* dare *to interfere with the important people.* She stopped to notify her aunt of their plans, and then Julia and Lizzy slipped out quickly before the other children could discover their plans.

"It's so hard being the oldest," Julia burst out once they were out of view of the house. "I have to be kind and patient and entertain them and be a model of good behavior and help them get over all of their problems. Well, what about when I have problems? What then?" She crossed her arms and kicked at a stray pebble in the road.

Lizzy opened her mouth to answer and stopped. Jane had always been such a perfect older sister that she had never considered all of the pressures that must come with it. Even now that she was old enough to try to purposely curb Lydia and Kitty's behavior, she always had Jane to fall back on for support or in frustration. What Jane must deal with, how she must feel beyond that perfect calm demeanor!

"I think you do a wonderful job with your brothers and sister," she told Julia after a pause. "And you have me here now for when you need to talk about your own problems."

Julia reached out and took her hand. They walked in silence for a while before Julia hung her head and told her boots, "I don't really have any problems. I'm just tired of always having to solve problems and be the nice one and never get mad."

Elizabeth laughed a bit. "It's an elder sister's prerogative to get mad now and then," she told her cousin. "I'm sure I've gotten mad at Mary or Kitty or Lydia countless times. You just can't be cruel. If they know they've done something wrong, they'll forgive you in time. It might even be good for them." Perhaps she should have gotten mad at Lydia a few more times for chasing after anything in breeches, Elizabeth reflected wryly.

Julia stopped suddenly and gave Elizabeth a tight, brief hug. "I'm glad you stayed here for Christmas," she said, voice full of feeling. She stepped back, hung her head, and then grabbed Lizzy's hand again. Elizabeth grasped her cousin's hand tightly and they walked on, talking about preparations for the upcoming Christmas celebrations.

Before long they came to Hyde Park and set off down one of its paths at random, still chatting. "Oh, I do wish we could run," Julia said longingly. Since she was half-skipping already, Elizabeth had no trouble believing her desire.

"I declare, I may have met my match at walking," she told Julia. "It's a shame we didn't bring William along—we could turn him loose and have the perfect excuse to chase after him."

Julia sighed. "Yes, but then he'd tire himself out and we'd have to carry him all the way home, and not get a single word in while he talked about the ducks and geese."

Elizabeth laughed. She had brought her youngest cousin to Hyde Park not two days before and experienced exactly such a situation. "He does do a rather impressively loud impression of a duck," she admitted. "That's one that even Lydia couldn't beat, although I think her pig impression still may be my favorite. Especially since she climbed into the pig pen wearing a brand new dress and actually rolled in the mud to 'be authentic,' as she told Mama."

Julia burst out laughing and doubled over, holding her sides. They were rounding a corner, and Lizzy was so focused on keeping her cousin upright that she nearly walked straight into a man coming from the other direction, not catching herself until the last second. Stumbling, she and Julia both would have fallen if not for a tight, annoyingly familiar grip on her elbows.

"Miss Elizabeth!" Miss Darcy's voice exclaimed.

Oh, dear Lord, no. Not him.

CHAPTER NINE

Lizzy blinked twice, hard, trying to clear her mind and vision. She looked up to see Georgiana's concerned face peering over her brother's shoulder. As she regained her focus, Elizabeth realized that Mr. Darcy still held her arm just above the elbow.

She forced herself to look up at him, praying that her face only *felt* like the color of ripe tomatoes. "I thank you, sir," she managed to say politely.

"Are you always so prone to falling, Miss Elizabeth?" Mr. Darcy asked, eyes unreadable as usual.

Elizabeth opened her mouth to snap, "Only around you," and then closed it again, unsure of how to proceed before their audience. "Not usually, sir," she replied instead, not quite managing to keep her tone polite. Stepping back to free herself from his grasp, Elizabeth caught sight of Georgiana and Julia's expressions. Georgiana looked concerned, while Julia's face showed simple curiosity.

"I was aware that you are quite fond of laughing, but I must confess I have not seen you do so to such an extent previously," Mr. Darcy said. He had not stepped back when she did, and still stood too close for her comfort. Elizabeth gritted her teeth and forced herself to stand still. She did not fully understand what Mr. Darcy was about, but could easily imagine that he assumed whomever he met would clear the way for him rather than moving himself. She would not give him the satisfaction of complying.

"I do not believe I have laughed myself into danger before, Mr. Darcy, but then I am generally in a location where gentlemen with which to collide are few and far between. The only dangers I face at home are trees and the occasional chicken that has escaped from its coop." And, of course, the danger of being labeled as silly as her younger sisters, but few people in Longbourn or Meryton would even think to consider such a possibility.

Turning purposefully to Georgiana, Elizabeth smiled more genuinely and said, "I believe you remember my cousin Julia, Miss Darcy?"

Julia dropped a shallow curtsey complete with a tiny wobble, glancing up sideways at Lizzy to make sure she had done the right thing.

Elizabeth gave her a small smile, and seeing that Georgiana was unsure of how to respond, went on. "Is it not a perfect day for a walk? Julia and I could not resist such wonderful weather."

Now Georgiana smiled and looked more sure of herself. "Oh, it is a wonderful day! William was good enough to accompany me since my companion is not feeling well. I do love being outside on a day like this."

Lizzy's eyes met Mr. Darcy's the moment that Georgiana remarked on her companion's health. She knew without a doubt that he was thinking, like her, of her accusation that the entire household was ill. Her cheeks burned again, and she dropped her gaze first.

"Shall we continue walking, Georgie?" Mr. Darcy asked. "If you want enough time to sketch we should move along soon."

"Oh—yes—of course," Georgiana said. She looked at Elizabeth almost expectantly, drew breath as if to speak, and then let it out again and took her brother's arm.

Lizzy turned towards her cousin, ready for Mr. Darcy to march his sister off in the opposite direction as fast as he could.

"Would you care to join us, Miss Elizabeth and Miss Gardiner?" he asked.

Julia blushed, not used to her official title, and Elizabeth stared stupidly at Mr. Darcy for a moment. Did he always have to keep her so off balance that thinking felt like she was trying to run through honey?

She glanced at Julia, half wishing that her cousin would give her a reason to decline the offer, but Julia looked quite excited. Turning back to the Darcys, Elizabeth focused on *Miss* Darcy and smiled genuinely at the young lady. "We would be delighted to join you."

They walked only a short distance more before they came upon a bench and a view that Georgiana deemed perfect to sketch. She settled herself on the bench with her sketchpad and Julia immediately sat down next to her to study her technique. Elizabeth, with only a passing interest in drawing, was left standing next to Mr. Darcy.

"I must admit that I am glad my cousin William is not here," Elizabeth said when the silence had at last become too much for her to bear.

"William is the youngest, correct?" Darcy inquired. At her nod, he added, "And why are you glad for his absence?"

"Because this peaceful scene would be far less so if William were present," Elizabeth said, chancing a look at him before turning back to her study of the ducks. "He is quite fond of yelling and racing straight at any animal in sight, especially birds. We were here recently, and when I picked him up to cut off opportunities for such activities, he spent the rest of our walk quacking and squawking in my ear. He's an adorable boy, but peaceful he is not."

To her surprise, Mr. Darcy chuckled. "I know what you mean."

She looked at him, startled, and he chuckled again.

"You wouldn't know it to look at her now, but Georgiana was hardly a calm, quiet child. She followed me for hours with countless questions, trying to do everything I did. She nearly killed herself trying to ride a green broke horse once when I didn't know she had escaped the nursery. I taught her to ride her pony so I wouldn't have to worry so much that she would fall off." He hesitated. "Do you ride, Miss Elizabeth?"

She looked back out at the water once again. "No. We had only plow horses at home, and I was not inclined to learn the few times I had the chance. I am but a poor country miss, Mr. Darcy. Walking as a form of transportation works well enough for me, even if I do get mud on my boots and dust on my hem."

There. She had said what he must be thinking, and would let him respond as he would.

But he said nothing. Finally, after half a minute of silence, she tried again, determined to not be intimidated by his demeanor. "Miss Darcy has certainly changed from the exuberant child that you describe."

"Yes," he responded. "She was only six when our mother died, and it curbed a great deal of her excitement. And then when—" he stopped abruptly, then continued in a different tone. "And then as she grew older, of course she learned to act as a young lady should."

Yes, of course, Mr. Darcy. She learned to act as my sisters did not.

"You have been good for her," Mr. Darcy added, and she could not stop herself from turning to stare at him.

"Me, Mr. Darcy? By all but running away from home and then insulting the gentleman good enough to help me on my spontaneous journey? I daresay you are thinking of someone else—anyone else but me."

He dropped his eyes and scuffed a perfectly shined boot on the dirt at their feet. "I owe you an apology, Miss Elizabeth."

She blinked and narrowed her eyes, unbelieving, but said nothing.

"I was wrong to chastise you as I did. You could not have known this, but you came to us on a most stressful day. Still, that does not excuse my poor manners, and I must beg your forgiveness for such thoughtlessness on my part."

She met his eyes and blinked, knowing her mouth had fallen slightly open in surprise and yet unable to compose herself.

"You *have* been good for Georgiana," he continued passionately. "Your liveliness has helped her lose some of the shyness she has struggled with throughout her adolescence, and I have noticed you help her through more than one conversation where she would have stayed silent if not for the encouragement. There is little I would not do for my sister, but I have been unable to help her as you do unthinkingly. So as well as apologizing, I must thank you as well."

Elizabeth was rendered utterly speechless for a moment. So even Mr. Darcy had a chink in his formidable armor, she mused. A pity the man was insufferable in every dealing that did not concern his sister.

Finally, she collected herself. "It is not only you who owes an apology, Mr. Darcy. I have been ashamed of my behavior since I left your house. It is your household to oversee and discipline as you will, and I was most certainly out of my place by speaking as I did. I am especially sorry if I brought any distress upon Miss Darcy, for she is a dear girl." She stopped, deciding it better to say less than to speak more than she ought. Oh, if only her mother could apply such a thought!

"Lizzy, come look!" Julia exclaimed, grinning at her from the bench. Georgiana blushed and looked shy, but smiled as well nonetheless. Elizabeth glanced at Mr. Darcy, unsure where their recent conversation left things. She hesitated a moment longer, then gave a short bob of a curtsey and went to exclaim over Georgiana's truly delightful sketch.

*

They parted ways at the exit to the park, the Darcys headed back to Grosvenor Square, and Lizzy and Julia turning towards Gracechurch Street. Elizabeth and Georgiana had made no more plans to see each other or even mentioned the possibility, so when a maid announced Mr. Darcy's arrival at the Gardiner's house several days after Christmas, Elizabeth had no idea what to think. She had been playing with William and Eleanor, and hurriedly called the governess to take over her charges. Stopping only to straighten her gown and hair in the hallway—damned if she'd let him catch her looking any more like a country girl than she already did— she hurried down the stairs to see what had brought her unexpected visitor.

Mrs. Gardiner was already in the parlor with Mr. Darcy when she arrived. He looked rather distressed, and her mind immediately flew to all sorts of dreadful events that could have brought him here. Forcing herself to push such thoughts aside, Elizabeth curtseyed and managed a greeting, then took a seat next to her aunt and looked expectantly at Mr. Darcy.

He colored slightly under her appraisal. "I must confess I have a rather unusual request," he began, looking down at his hands folded in his lap before continuing. "But I have an idea and was loathe to think of anyone better suited to help me than the two of you."

At his words, Elizabeth relaxed slightly. Her aunt was here as more than a chaperone, then. Heaven forbid that Darcy should call on only her.

"What can we do for you, Mr. Darcy?" Mrs. Gardiner asked, smiling.

"You may have heard that my sister, Georgiana, will soon have a birthday. She will turn seventeen. I have been thinking of hosting a party for her, and thought her birthday may provide a reasonable excuse. She will not come out until next season or the following one, whichever she prefers, so it need not be a large, formal party. That is what brought me here. I know several people who would be happy to orchestrate a ball or other large event where Georgiana would feel uncomfortable with the crowd. I thought that perhaps the two of you could help me design a simpler, but more enjoyable celebration for her."

Ah, yes, come to the country miss for a simple party, when Caroline Bingley must be dying to organize Miss Darcy's birthday ball, Elizabeth thought. But still, she could not help but admit that he showed true understanding and care for his sister by requesting the party that he did. She would be far happier in a smaller, informal group than at any grand event.

"We should be delighted," Mrs. Gardiner said, after glancing at her niece to ascertain any dislike of the idea.

"I have a list of Georgiana's likes and dislikes," Mr. Darcy said, holding out a sheet of paper. "Perhaps it will not be helpful, but I could contribute at least this much. And of course I will cover any expenses," he added.

Mrs. Gardiner reached out and took the paper. "One cannot be too prepared, Mr. Darcy. Thank you for your list."

Elizabeth leaned over to look. Some things she had already known Georgiana to be fond of—piano, drawing, walks, intimate groups. Others, like museums, trips to the theater, and dancing, also in small parties, were new to her.

They had been discussing different ideas for a quarter of an hour or so when the door opened and a maid stepped in. "Beg pardon, but two letters just arrived for Miss Elizabeth. From Hertfordshire."

Lizzy stood immediately and went to the door to take her letters from the maid. Both were from Jane, though the first was written so hastily that the address was barely legible. Elizabeth frowned. What could make Jane write so, when normally her handwriting was as gorgeous as the rest of her? Jane's last letter had spoken of improving health, but that had been several days ago. She looked up, frowning. "Aunt—"

"Yes, Lizzy, of course," Mrs. Gardiner said without waiting to hear the end of the request. "I know you are anxious for word from home."

Mr. Darcy glanced up as well. "Is something amiss?" he asked.

"Several members of my family fell ill just before Christmas," she told him as she made her way to a sunny seat placed by a window specifically for letter reading. "Last I heard their conditions are all improving, but I have had no word in several days."

She sat down and tore open the first letter, anxiously scanning its contents. The first half was promising, speaking of great improvements in the health of Kitty and Mrs. Bennet, although Mary continued to spend a great deal of her time resting. There was mention of a small party at Lucas Lodge that Jane and Lydia had attended, since both were completely healthy again. The second half of the letter, though, made Elizabeth gasp in shock and despair.

Flashes of the letter jumped out at her— *something has occurred of a most unexpected and serious nature… all well… poor Lydia… gone off to Scotland… Wickham!*

"No," Elizabeth whispered to herself. She squeezed her eyes shut for a moment, caught between flinging the letter away and reading it to the conclusion. Curiosity won out, and she looked back to see what else the letter contained. None of it was better, and it said little that Lizzy couldn't have guessed. Jane hoped for a marriage, Mrs. Bennet was in a sad condition, Lydia had little money—certainly nothing to tempt the man who had once hoped to receive Georgiana's thirty thousand pounds.

She cast the letter away and snatched up the second, opening it with far more urgency than she had the first. She scanned it again, heart sinking further still when it only confirmed her fears. ...*I have bad news for you, and it cannot be delayed. Imprudent as a marriage between Mr. Wickham and our poor Lydia would be, we are now anxious to be assured it has taken place, for there is but too much reason to fear they are not gone to Scotland.* Of course they have not! He is a scoundrel, and she a fool!

Elizabeth raced through the rest of the letter, although she had to read it three times before the meaning truly sank in. They were not gone to Scotland, but London was suspected—yes, she could believe that. Colonel Foster found Wickham a man not to be trusted. Smart man, smart man— but why could he have not minded Lydia better! Mrs. Bennet indisposed, of course she is, when is she not when anything distressing occurs? And Mr. Bennet, finally affected, when it was far too late to have an effect on his daughter.

Finally, at the end of the letter, she found something to grasp onto. Mr. Bennet coming to London, requesting Mr. Gardiner's assistance—yes, perhaps her uncle could succeed where her father would flounder, for what did he know of London? She looked up to find Mrs. Gardiner and Mr. Darcy staring at her, the first with concern and the latter, shock. "Aunt—my uncle, please fetch my uncle at once."

Mrs. Gardiner opened her mouth—to query, to protest? —and then closed it again. She stood and was gone, moving purposely out of the room to find her husband.

CHAPTER TEN

"Miss Elizabeth! What is the matter?" Mr. Darcy asked when the door had closed on her aunt.

She shook her head blindly, all rational thought having left her.

"Let me call you a maid, or a glass of wine—shall I get you one?"

"No, no, I am well, truly," she said forcing herself to focus on his face, or at least close enough to its general vicinity to convince him. "I—I am just distressed by some horrible news I have received from Longbourn." She swallowed hard, clenching her hands into fists on her lap as if to hold onto her control, and then burst into tears.

He stood and took two long strides towards her before seeming to remember the proprieties that overlay even the most desperate of occurrences. Halting abruptly, he twisted his long fingers together and stared down at her, concern written across his face.

"Here," Elizabeth said in a choked voice when she could at last speak again, holding out the second letter, which she still held. "You may as well know all. It cannot be kept quiet for long. My youngest—my baby sister Lydia—" another sob escaped her and several seconds passed before she could continue. "She has run off, attempted to

elope, with Mr. Wickham. You know him too well
to doubt my fears. I have no hope. She is gone, lost
to us forever, and we shall all be forced to pay for
what she has done. Stupid, headstrong girl!

"I could have prevented this," Elizabeth
continued in a whisper. "I told Jane—I *told* her—
that he was not to be trusted, not what we were lead
to believe, to be careful—but when has Jane
believed poorly of anyone? If I had not run off and
abandoned my sisters to save my own foolish,
wounded pride, this may never had happened. I can
blame no one but myself." Tears streaked down her
face, but she did not begin to sob again.

"That is distressing news indeed," Mr. Darcy
said, once he had scanned the letter and handed it
back to her. "Are you sure, absolutely certain, that
things stand as you believe?"

"Oh yes. You read what Jane wrote. They are
not gone to Scotland, that much is sure, and she has
nothing to tempt him for long. My father will come
to search for her, but I have no hope for his success.
Perhaps my uncle may offer some assistance, but
what is to be done even if they are found? He
cannot wish to marry her, and they *must* marry if
any of our reputations are to be salvaged."

Darcy turned and began to pace, and for a brief
moment of respite, Elizabeth recalled Mr. Bingley
teasing him, during one of those long rainy days at
Netherfield, about his habit to pace when troubled.

It seemed a lifetime ago to her now. There would be no more trips to Netherfield now, no visits with Mr. Bingley even if he were to return. They would be social outcasts, pariahs, examples held up to other young ladies as the harm that one sister could do to all.

He turned back halfway through a stride, face stern, and Elizabeth saw one more thing that she should lose—the friendship of Miss Darcy, who had already become dear to her. Mr. Darcy would never allow his precious sister to associate with a fallen family, and certainly not one now tied irrevocably to the man who had courted, seduced, and assaulted her.

"Oh, do conceal the awful truth from Miss Darcy, as long as it may be done," Elizabeth burst out before he could speak. "Let this awful affair not hurt another young lady more than it ultimately must."

His face softened for a moment, then hardened again into a mask. "I shall do that, Miss Elizabeth, for your sake as well as my sister's. You are too good to think of her feelings at such a time."

She looked up and met his eyes squarely, for once not bothered by his cool demeanor. This vexing man would also be gone from her life now, and she could only feel remorse where she would have expected relief. There would be no more intriguing conversations to puzzle over later, no games of wit—certainly no requests for help planning a sister's birthday.

He broke their eye contact first. "I fear you have long been wishing me gone, Miss Elizabeth, and indeed I can claim no right to remain save real concern and regret. I too could have taken steps to change this outcome had I not feared for my sister's reputation in a town she is likely never to visit again. It is your sister who will now pay the price of my silence, and I must offer you my sincerest apologies. I hope that a happy outcome can yet be found. Good day, Miss Elizabeth."

He quitted the room, passing her aunt and uncle as they entered. He gave a brief bow to both and then was gone.

"Elizabeth, what happened?" Mr. Gardiner burst out as both Gardiners hurried across the room to her. In response, she handed over the letters, unsure she could bear having to tell the story again. Her uncle snatched them and read hurriedly, his wife peering over his shoulder.

"This Wickham fellow, do you know him?" Mr. Gardiner asked when he reached the end of the first letter.

Elizabeth gave a short nod, bracing herself for the questions that would surely follow, and the answers she must give.

"Will he marry her? Is he the type to stay true to his word?

"No," she said with enough vehemence to surprise herself. "No, he will not and he certainly is not." Speaking in general terms and being sure not to reveal the young lady in question, she revealed what she had learned of the man just prior to her removal from Hertfordshire.

"It was not you, surely?" her uncle asked with considerable alarm when she had finished.

Elizabeth flushed. "No. He paid me attentions, and I encouraged him perhaps more than I ought to have, but there was nothing inappropriate about his manner towards me." *Nothing other than a desire to poison her against a man who had done nothing but try to help him and had been treated despicably in return.*

She had told her aunt, but not her uncle, of Mr. Collins' proposal and now explained briefly, saying, "My reason for leaving Longbourn was unwanted advances in the form of a most misguided proposal, but it came from my cousin Mr. Collins, not Mr. Wickham. He may be a most undesirable husband, but he was at least honest in his advances and intents."

Mr. Gardiner gave a short nod and continued reading. Mrs. Gardiner, who had continued to scan the letter throughout her husband's short conversation with Elizabeth, stood. "I shall prepare a room for Mr. Bennet, and warn the children that his visit will not be for pleasure. Oh!" she exclaimed. "Mr. Darcy! He must have been most put out by this afternoon's events."

"Do not worry, Aunt," Elizabeth said woodenly. "*That* is all settled, and he shall not hold it against us any more than is to be expected given Lydia's actions."

Her aunt's jaw dropped in astonishment and she seemed ready to launch into several questions of her own. Elizabeth was saved—for it was certain that her aunt's interpretation of the matter tended incorrectly towards matrimony—by her uncle finishing the second letter.

"Of course I shall assist Mr. Bennet in any way I can," he said. "Come to my study, Lizzy, and tell me all that you know of this man. Perhaps his past comments to you will reveal something we can use to find him and Lydia."

*

By the time Mr. Bennet arrived, dusty and ruffled from the hurried journey, Elizabeth had recounted everything she could recall about Mr. Wickham to her uncle. Little had come of the exercise, but it had dried Lizzy's tears. She was not one to be sad or melodramatic for long, and her thoughts now were focused on collecting every bit of information she could, starting with her father.

Mr. Bennet answered the first several questions that she fired at him, then sighed tiredly. "Let me speak with your uncle, Lizzy. Jane said she wrote you with more information, and we have gathered nothing of significance since then. I looked for them in Epsom and Clapham and have had no sign of them. London remains our best hope."

Clenching her teeth in frustration—here was yet another reason to hate being female—she left her uncle's study and went directly to her room to write Jane, who must surely be carrying all of the responsibilities at home, with an absent father and mother in need of constant care and attention. Oh, how she wished she could be there to help her sister! At home she could be doing far more good than here.

Dearest Jane,

   My father has arrived and is locked away with my uncle. Your letter came not long before he arrived. I believe my uncle already has several men out looking for W and L discretely, although I cannot say for sure. My father found no word of them at Epson or Clapham and has had little chance to do more as of yet. I wish I had more real news for you, but as my father and uncle are still formulating their plans and I am not allowed in discussions, I can give you little reassurance at this time. I will only say that my uncle is not without hope.

I dearly wish I could be at home with you, dearest sister. Please keep me updated on any arrangements there. I know you will handle everything with far more patience than I could hope to muster, but I must say I am worried for you. Let Mary and Kitty take their turns with Mama, and see if Mrs. Hill can mix up the tonic she makes to help with Mama's nerves.

Here I am, telling you things you surely know as well as I do. I must give worry as my excuse. But Jane, I must ask you to do one other thing, and I know you shall not like it. Do question Kitty to see if she knows any details, even ones that seem insignificant, about where L might go or what she may have planned to do. You must make it clear to her

*that a single word could be what
leads us to Lydia.*

*I shall end here, for I know you
must be busy. I will write again as
soon as there is any news to relate.*

Your loving sister,

Elizabeth

The next few days left all the main inhabitants of
the Gardiner's house harried and tired. Letters were
exchanged with Colonel Foster, although they
produced virtually no clues about his location. Mr.
Wickham's character sank even lower in the eyes of
the Gardiners and Bennets as they learned more and
more about activities and debts he had hidden
previously. Finally, tired and discouraged, Mr.
Bennet turned the rest of the search over to Mr.
Gardiner and departed for Longbourn.

Upon hearing news of this plan, Elizabeth
immediately began packing to accompany him, only
to be stopped shortly by her father.

"Lizzy, you would do me a great favor to stay
here while there is still a chance that Lydia will be
discovered. Should your uncle learn of her
whereabouts, you may be able to help recover her,
and I trust that information will pass between

yourself and Jane far faster than your uncle or I could communicate. Will you do this for me?

Having been left out of nearly all the meetings of the past days, Elizabeth could not help but be touched by her father's request. She readily agreed, on the condition that he delay his departure until she could send a note for Jane, who surely was expecting her sister's eminent return.

The next morning Mr. Bennet was gone, and Elizabeth found herself sitting next to her aunt in the sitting room as she had been on the day when the letters first arrived.

"Well, Lizzy, I had thought we might attend a ball or a play at the theatre to get our fill of drama, but I must say I am rather ready for a happy ending and at least a sennight with no excitement at all. This affair has provided more drama than I ever hoped to see."

"A sennight?" Elizabeth asked. "I was thinking a year would be preferable, but at least a fortnight. Although at this point I would settle for having the happy ending."

Her aunt sighed. "Yes, I would be more than satisfied with that as well. Poor Lydia."

"Poor Lydia? When she is at least half to blame for this situation in the first place?"

"Poor Lydia," Mrs. Gardiner repeated. "For while it may have been her idea, or at least an idea she agreed with, she has been removed from her family and friends with no means to ever return. She is in the midst of a scheme that she cannot fully understand, and may not understand for quite some time. Lydia is still a child, for all that she is headstrong and excitable and irresponsible."

It was Lizzy's turn to sigh. She had managed to keep her emotions in check for the past week by focusing on Lydia's contributions to the problem, rather than the situation that she must now find herself in. Her aunt's words threatened to break through that control.

A figure passing in front of the window caught her attention, and for a moment all thoughts of her sister fled Elizabeth's mind. She simply stared, transfixed, as her uncle walked by, talking intently to a tall, dark-haired gentleman with a stern countenance.

"Aunt," she queried, barely aware of what she said, "What in the world is Mr. Darcy doing here?"

CHAPTER ELEVEN

Elizabeth was not to discover the reason for Mr. Darcy's presence immediately, much to her chagrin. The two men locked themselves in Mr. Gardiner's study. Lunch was delivered, followed by tea sometime later, but the men themselves did not emerge. Only when it was time for dinner did they at last quit the study.

From her seat near the sitting room door, chosen exactly for such a purpose, Elizabeth heard their voices sound in the hall and sprang up. She faltered at the sitting room door, unsure of how to proceed or what her reception would be, but in the end curiosity won out and she pulled the door open, breathing quickly with nerves and anticipation.

The men stopped talking upon seeing her, and for several seconds Elizabeth found her eyes locked with Mr. Darcy's.

"Lizzy, perhaps you can succeed where I have failed," Mr. Gardiner said, either unaware or purposely uncaring of the tension between the two. "Mr. Darcy is convinced that he would be an imposition at our table this evening, though I have assured him such is not the case."

The comment called her back to herself, and Elizabeth dropped a short curtsey to both men. "I am sure Mr. Darcy is capable of making up his own mind, and I shall not endeavor to change his opinions, for I have known him long enough to think it a futile task," she said with far more poise than she felt.

Mr. Darcy frowned, causing Lizzy to smile slightly. He must despise her by association now, but it was somehow comforting that his stern, taciturn nature had not changed. When all else failed, she could count on him to disapprove.

"You seem certain, madam," he replied coolly.

"I am. Though if you find such a thought disconcerting, you are most welcome to prove me wrong and join us for dinner this evening, sir. We would welcome your presence at the table." *And perhaps you will answer some of my questions, or at least hint to the answers!*

Darcy smiled. "Are you challenging me, Miss Elizabeth?"

"I am," she replied readily. "Go on, Mr. Darcy, the choice is yours. Stay unsociable and stubborn, or accept my uncle's invitation and claim the victory."

"I had not thought you so willing to manipulate," he said, raising an eyebrow.

A servant came up to speak to Mr. Gardiner, and Darcy and Elizabeth were momentarily left alone in the conversation. The lack of observation made her bold, and she answered, "Perhaps not usually, Mr.

109

Darcy, but I must admit that the last week has taken a toll on my usual spirits. I shall soon go mad if I am not provided some distraction from my own thoughts."

His frown returned in force, but rather than turning to leave as she had half expected, he responded, "Yes, I must say I know the feeling. Very well, then, Miss Elizabeth, I shall accept the invitation."

"You are too kind, sir," she said. "I thank you, and give you my promise that not a single person at the dinner table shall bring up money, marriage, or officers in any way that should offend you."

He started, obviously surprised at her forwardness, and stood staring at her in shock.

Smiling, Elizabeth dropped a deeper curtsey. "Excuse me, sir. I must go inform my aunt of the addition to our family party and then change for dinner." Turning on her heel, she walked off, feeling much better than she had during the past few days. Yes, having Mr. Darcy as her verbal fencing partner for the evening would be quite distracting, indeed. Let him hate her if he would; the more intricate the conversation, the more likely she was to forget Lydia and her pending ruin for a few moments throughout the evening.

Dinner passed pleasantly. Removed from the vulgar conversation of Mrs. Bennet, Mr. Darcy

relaxed more than Elizabeth had ever seen.
Elizabeth watched him to see if he was put off by
her uncle's business in trade, but saw nothing to
suggest that Darcy did not consider him an equal. If
there had been any tense moments between the
gentlemen, they had obviously been addressed and
were now left in the past.

Mrs. Gardiner took the opportunity to question
Mr. Darcy, not on his wealth and social standing,
but on any updates from Lambton that he had
neglected to tell her during their previous discussion
on the matter. They spoke of Napoleon and the
war, of a show the Gardiners and Mr. Darcy had
both attended, of how the weather differed between
London, Hertfordshire, and Derbyshire. To Lizzy's
frustration, not one word was said about what had
taken place all day in Mr. Gardiner's study. Only
when they rose from the table did she catch a hint.

"Thank you for the meal and company, but I
really must be going now." He exchanged looks
with Mr. Gardiner, who nodded solemnly.

"Give our regards to your sister," Mrs. Gardiner
said.

"She shall be happy to receive them," Mr. Darcy
replied. Several more pleasantries were exchanged,
and then he disappeared into the night.

"Well, dear," Mrs. Gardiner looked at her
husband once Mr. Darcy had gone, "are you going

to tell us what had you barricaded behind closed doors all day?"

Mr. Gardiner hesitated, rubbing his chin with one hand while he thought. "I would say nothing, but I know that neither of you will deal with curiosity easily. Very well then. Most of what we discussed is not mine to repeat, but Mr. Darcy has expressed the belief that he may be able to locate Mr. Wickham, and with him Lydia."

"Why would he do that?" Lizzy burst out. "He hates Mr. Wickham, and Mr. Wickham feels the same about him!"

Mr. Gardiner frowned slightly at his niece. "He believes that his silence on Mr. Wickham's character in Meryton contributed directly to Lydia's situation."

"She wouldn't have listened to him," Elizabeth said confidently, causing both her aunt and uncle to frown this time.

"No, but perhaps Colonel Foster would have paid more attention to his activities and companions," Mr. Gardiner said. It was a fair point, and Elizabeth conceded it as such.

"He also feels a more personal connection to the affair," Mr. Gardiner continued, causing both women to look at him sharply. He met Elizabeth's eyes squarely. "He detailed more of the circumstances under which you became acquainted with his sister."

She nodded her understanding, and as Mr. Gardiner refused to say another word, the conversation came abruptly to an end.

*

The next day passed slowly. The entire house seemed to be waiting for something, although most of the inhabitants had no idea what that might be, and it was a most uncomfortable sensation. The children fussed and fought; the servants whispered about what might be keeping Mr. Gardiner home when it was his custom to visit his warehouses. Elizabeth attempted to read and gave up at least half a dozen times.

Partway through the afternoon, a message arrived, though not the one that they had been waiting for. A worker had fallen and been injured at one of Mr. Gardiner's warehouses, and he was needed immediately. He departed in a matter of minutes, taking Mrs. Gardiner with him in case her assistance was needed. Elizabeth, seeing them off, thought that her aunt had jumped at the chance to actually *do* something other than wait, but made no comment. Had it been proper, she most likely would have done the same.

Her aunt and uncle had been gone for nearly an hour when Lizzy, who had retreated to the nursery to distract herself if at all possible, caught sight of Mr. Darcy passing in front of the house in the street below. Dashing down the stairs, she met him in the front hallway with wide, questioning eyes.

"Is Mr. Gardiner at home?" he asked immediately.

"No," Elizabeth answered. "He was called away just recently to attend to an accident at one of his warehouses and took my aunt with him. They planned to stay until the man had been given all the care he needed, and I do not know when to expect him home."

Mr. Darcy opened his mouth and snapped it closed with such energy that Lizzy wondered if he had bitten off a curse. He took a moment to collect himself, then studied her with an assessing gaze. "Do you have any influence over your sister?"

"You found her."

"Elizabeth," he admonished curtly.

She blinked, startled by the use of her Christian name as much as by his scolding tone of voice. He raised his eyebrows, giving no apologies for the breach of propriety.

"I don't know. I would like to say yes, but Lydia has always been headstrong and likely to do something simply because she was told she ought not. If she is set in her path and feels no guilt or fear, attempting to persuade her into doing anything may backfire."

"Would your uncle have any better luck? Your aunt?"

"Perhaps my uncle, but likely not my aunt."

"Very well," Darcy said, seeming to make up his mind. He lowered his voice. "I do not like to do this, but it may be our only chance. I know where your sister and Mr. Wickham are lodged, but was informed that they leave tonight. I do not know if that is true or not, but will not take the chance if I can help it. Whatever Lydia's response to you, I fear it would be worse if I were to go alone, and as your uncle is not here I—"

"Let me fetch my pelisse," Lizzy said breathlessly, already turning to run up to her room for the garment.

He caught hold of her arm. "I do not dare bring a servant for fear of the truth leaking out. You would go alone with me and accept the risk of what may be said if we are seen?"

She looked up at him. "If I do not go, if we cannot recover my sister, then I am already ruined. If that must be my situation, I should like to own the blame for it, Mr. Darcy."

He maintained his grip for a moment, eyes searching her face as if checking for the truth of the statement. Then he nodded once and released her. "Very well. Fetch your coat, and leave a few words for your aunt and uncle. Then we must go."

She nodded in return and left him. Her tasks were accomplished in a matter of minutes, and then Elizabeth found herself being hastily handed up into a much smaller, shabbier carriage than she would have expected Mr. Darcy to own and use.

"It is an old carriage, but one I thought better suited to our task," he said as he climbed in after her and settled himself on the opposite seat.

"It concerns me, sir, that you were able to guess so accurately what I was thinking," she said, turning her head slightly and raising an eyebrow. "Do tell, what is your secret?"

"You have an expressive face," Mr. Darcy responded shortly, pulling back the curtain at the window slightly rather than meeting her eyes. "And it was an easy assumption to make, given what I know of your curiosity."

"Am I so easy to understand, then?" she pressed, leaning back against the seat. Elizabeth did not like that idea. Jane understood her expressions, but then Jane had been her constant companion and confidant since she was old enough to speak. That Mr. Darcy should understand her even partially as well made her uneasy, though she could not say exactly why.

"I daresay not to most people," he replied. "I have had the advantage of observing you in several situations where you had ample reason to mask your true feelings, at least to the degree required for social graces and civility." At her narrowed eyes, he went on, "Your dance with Mr. Collins was one, and a good deal of the time you spent in Miss Bingley's company at Netherfield comes to mind as well."

Lizzy felt one corner of her mouth quirk up in spite of herself. "If you were looking to make a study of my expressions, Mr. Darcy, I agree that those situations lend themselves nicely to the occasion. I suppose I shall have to resign myself to your knowledge."

"And what of your own knowledge?" Mr. Darcy asked. "Have you had any success in understanding my character?"

Elizabeth's mind flashed back to the ball at Netherfield where this conversation had originated. How she had berated him about his treatment of Mr. Wickham then, believing Darcy to be the cruel one and Mr. Wickham the poorly treated innocent! Must she always berate Mr. Darcy where it was neither called for nor polite? What he must think of her now!

She drew slightly into herself, making sure no one could see her through the inch-wide strip of open window exposed through the curtains. "I must say, Mr. Darcy, that some things have changed little since the last time we spoke of characters. You still puzzle me exceedingly, though the information comes less from others now and more from my own observations."

He gave his signature frown and opened his mouth to answer, but at that moment the carriage jolted, swerving to miss something or someone. Mr. Darcy's hand shot out to steady Elizabeth, but she had already taken a firm grip on her seat and was in no danger of falling. Sliding across the bench and peering out a corner of the window, she made out a woman yelling at the carriage driver, two ragged children clutching her skirts and another in her arms. Lizzy pursed her lips, but took heart in the fact that none of the party seemed harmed.

The carriage was drawing onto streets that housed less reputable establishments and shabbier houses. They had traveled through such neighborhoods in silence for several minutes when Mr. Darcy reached up and rapped twice on the top of the carriage. It slowed, then stopped in front of an especially shabby inn.

"Lydia is *here*?" Lizzy heard herself ask plaintively. She had guessed that Mr. Wickham would come to such a place to hide, but seeing it was different than suspecting. For the first time in days, she felt truly sorry for her youngest sister and struggled to hold back the hot tears that pricked her eyes.

Darcy reached out and put a hand on her knee, then pulled it back instantly when she jerked in surprise. "I'm sorry, I meant no disrespect, Miss Elizabeth." He opened the curtain slightly wider and indicated another inn two houses down. "Your sister is there, or at least Mr. Wickham and a young lady who matched her description were there earlier today. I did not want to alert him by pulling up directly in front of the establishment. As old as it is, this carriage is finer than many who would stay at such a place have."

He drew breath again, but Elizabeth stopped him with a look. "If you mean to tell me to stay in the carriage while you go in, save your breath, sir. Did you not bring me here to help with my sister however I could? I cannot help by hiding in a carriage halfway down the block."

To her extreme surprise, Darcy chuckled slightly. "I daresay you have made improvements on understanding my character, Miss Elizabeth." His frown returned, and he sighed. "Very well, then, I cannot deny that I did ask you for assistance. I will, however, insist that you obey whatever I should tell you to do once we are out of this carriage. I shall try to not make impossible requests, or even difficult ones. But I require your promise now that you shall do as I say, when I say.

I do not know what situation we are going into, and will not put you in any more danger than I must."

The request rankled, and Lizzy could see Mr. Darcy flinch slightly as he finished voicing the request, as if expecting her to throw it back in his face and flounce out of the carriage. Unfortunately, she could see his point, and it was her turn to sigh. "Very well, Mr. Darcy. I will promise to do what you say until we recover my sister and I am returned to my uncle's home."

He raised an eyebrow, obviously catching the limits that she had placed on the promise, but said nothing. "Then let us go."

Chapter Twelve

The sun had nearly set while they made their
way across London, and so Lizzy and Mr. Darcy
stepped out of the carriage into the falling dusk.
They exited the carriage on the side towards the
street so no one from the inn where Mr. Wickham
had been found could see them. Darcy, having
dealt with his old friend's tricks before, knew all too
well that a maid or the inn's proprietress could be
on watch for anyone who might not belong. A
single word to Wickham, and the search would
begin anew.

Elizabeth glanced up at the darkening sky with
worry in her eyes. "You said they may depart
today? What if we are too late?"

He looked up at the sky as well, then down into
her worried face. "I do not think Wickham would
change his lodging before true dark has fallen. He
has played this game before, and learned to be sly
and cautious in his ways."

Taking a small step closer to her, Mr. Darcy
lowered his head towards Elizabeth's ear. "It will
go better if we can pass as, well, together. If we are
standoffish and formal, someone may guess that not
is all as it seems."

She met his eyes, searching them for—what?
Lizzy wondered to herself. Dislike or not, she
trusted this man to not take advantage of her. "Is

this why you asked me about my willingness to bend propriety, Mr. Darcy?" she asked.

A pained look crossed his face and he moved a half step farther away. "I would not ask it if I did not feel it necessary."

Elizabeth took a deep breath and thought of Lydia, maybe concealed only yards away. There was little she wouldn't do at the moment to save her sister. Reaching out, Elizabeth laid her hand on Mr. Darcy's arm. "You did just secure my promise for obedience, sir. You need only order and I shall obey."

He looked as if he would say more, but she stepped forward, moving them past the single horse and into what dim light remained on the street. Soon the only light would come from lanterns by the doors.

Elizabeth's legs trembled slightly as they climbed the worn steps to the porch of the inn, but her head felt clear. Still, she was glad for the warmth and steadiness that Mr. Darcy's arm provided, even when he took her hand and tucked it into a clingier, less proper grip on his arm. She could go back to being proper Miss Elizabeth Bennet tomorrow—tonight she had a role to play, and she was glad to not have to play it alone.

Mr. Darcy knocked, and after what seemed like a heart-rendingly long time to Lizzy, a woman opened it. She immediately started in surprise when she recognized Mr. Darcy and would have slammed the door had he not got one booted foot stuck between the door and the frame.

Darcy shoved the door back open, causing the woman to stagger backwards. "Hello, Mrs. Younge," he said, voice cold. "I believe you know why I'm here."

She opened her mouth to yell, but Mr. Darcy was quicker. He held two gold guineas up in front of her face, his own expression seemingly carved from ice. Mrs. Younge froze, eyes on the money.

Elizabeth, who now stood half behind Mr. Darcy, wracked her brain for who Mrs. Younge could be. Only when Mrs. Younge's lips turned up in a sneer and said, "And how is Miss Darcy doing?" did she remember what Georgiana had told her on their way to London. Mrs. Younge had been the companion who encouraged her near elopement with Mr. Wickham. No wonder Darcy had been able to find him here, knowing what he did of their past.

"My sister is none of your concern," Darcy bit out. He shifted slightly more in front of Elizabeth, as if sensing her intense desire to say, "*My* sister is."

Unfortunately, Mrs. Younge also noticed the shift, and her eyes darted to Elizabeth. "You've a pretty one here, Mr. Darcy, although certainly not the type I would have expected to see you with. I wouldn't have called you good enough for him, miss," she added to Elizabeth in a conspiratorial tone. "Nothing against you, of course, but he's always been too high and mighty for us everyday folks."

Mr. Darcy tensed even more, and Lizzy realized she'd painted a very similar picture of him before—to his face, nonetheless. She arched an eyebrow at Mrs. Younge. "He can be rather stern until you get to know him, I'll give you that, but I've never seen him treat anyone less than fairly," she replied. "I'm sure you'd agree, Mrs. Younge."

The woman's expression soured. "How much did you pay this one to stand up for you, *Mister* Darcy, for not a single honest soul that I've met will do so."

"Enough, Mrs. Younge," Darcy. "I've heard enough from you at the moment. You'll have these guineas and more, but you'll do what I ask of you first."

The woman snorted, but her eyes strayed back to the coins that Darcy still held in plain sight, following them until they disappeared back into his pocket.

She looked up and glared. "And what is it you'll be asking of me this evening?"

"Mr. Wickham. Is he here?"

"What does it matter if he is?" Mrs. Younge retorted. "Have you not subjected the both of us to enough vile treatment?"

Darcy shrugged and went to turn on his heel, eliciting a noise rather like a cat's hiss from Mrs. Younge. "Fine," she spat out. He's here, but there had better be more money in it for me!"

Elizabeth schooled her face to show none of her thoughts, noticing that Mr. Darcy was having no trouble doing the same. Perhaps the lack of emotion he had shown in Hertfordshire was a learned trait.

"If you want more money," Mr. Darcy said calmly, "then you'll have to give us more information."

Mrs. Younge scowled at him, but made no protest.

"Is anyone with him?"

Mrs. Younge gave a long-suffering sigh. "There's a young lady with him, although I can't say he seemed too impressed with her. Very badly mannered, she was. He was so much happier with Georgiana. I still don't see why—" she stopped, looking directly up into Mr. Darcy's face as he stepped forward and loomed over her.

"Ten guineas. You will lead us up to his room, giving him no advanced warning, and then stay out of the matter completely."

"I'm not sure that's really worth it for me," Mrs. Younge said to Elizabeth's amazement.

Surprisingly, the comment seemed to calm Darcy rather than incensing him. He leaned back slightly, frowning at Mrs. Younge rather than attempting to intimidate her. "Fifteen. Take it now, or we will leave and you'll get nothing."

Mrs. Younge huffed, then put out her hand. Mr. Darcy counted ten guineas into her palm. At her outraged look, he held up one finger. "I don't trust you, Mrs. Younge. You'll get the rest when you follow through with the rest of our deal."

"As it happens, I don't trust you either, Mr. Darcy."

He cut her off. "You stand to gain five guineas by waiting patiently. I give you my word as a gentleman that I will honor our deal if you do the same."

With a final sneer, Mrs. Young stepped out from in front of the stairs. "Second floor, third door on the right. If you break something, you pay for it."

Darcy nodded once, then gestured for Elizabeth to go up the stairs and followed close behind her. "Quiet," he murmured when they reached the top of the stairs. "I don't trust her to not have notified him of my arrival. And I don't trust him to not try something desperate."

She nodded her understanding and stepped aside so he could go first down the dimly lit hallway, both of them moving softly. At the third door on the right, Mr. Darcy stopped and rapped on the door briskly, standing slightly to one side of the frame so the inhabitants would have to open the door more than a crack to see him.

There was no question of Mr. Wickham trying to flee, it turned out. He opened the door wide, showing a room nearly as dingy as the hallway with articles of clothing strewn across the floor and two bottles sitting on the small table. "Darcy, my friend," Wickham slurred, tripping over a shoe on the floor and grabbing the door frame to stay upright. "Have you come to join the party?"

"Who's there?" a muffled female voice asked from inside the room. The blankets on the bed were thrown back and Lydia's tousled head became visible—along with a good amount of her body. Lizzy sucked in a breath through her teeth at the sight of her sister, digging her fingernails into her palm to keep from exclaiming. Lydia wore only her chemise, and that had been loosened considerably.

"Not you!" she said in an annoyed tone as her eyes landed on Mr. Darcy. "Go away; you'll just make everything unpleasant if you stay. My dear Wickham is far better company than *you*."

"Lydia, have you no shame at all?" Elizabeth exclaimed, her patience finally worn through. "Cover yourself!"

For a second Lydia's eyes turned large and shocked as she swung her head to locate her sister, nearly concealed where she stood behind Mr. Darcy's broad shoulders. "Lizzy, what are you doing here?" she asked, her tone of bravado slipping halfway through the question.

"I've come to make sure you get home," Elizabeth responded firmly. On occasion, even Lydia would go along with the rational option if it was presented to her as the only one.

This time, her attempt failed. "Home, fah!" Lydia burst out. "Why should I want to go home? Nothing ever happens there, and now even the officers are gone—and Mr. Bingley! There will be no balls, no distractions or intrigues or anything interesting at all! Just day after day listening to Mary play her awful songs on the piano and trying to come up with *anything* to pass the time."

"Anything like running away with a man who doesn't really care for you?" Lizzy asked viciously.

"Of course he loves me! Don't you, dearest Wickham?"

"Then why did he try to elope with two other young ladies in the past year? I'm surprised he chose you, since he must know Father can give you next to nothing. Your thousand pounds is nothing compared to your dear Mr. Wickham's debts."

Lizzy had been watching Mr. Wickham as she spoke, and the looks that crossed his face told her two things: he did not care for her sister, and he had not known just how small her dowry was.

Elizabeth looked back at her sister. "Did you tell him what you had?" she asked Lydia directly.

"Of course I told him! He asked, and so I said that Mama has five thousand pounds, and that is where my dowry comes from."

"And you let him believe that all five thousand of that would be yours when you married?"

"No!" Lydia exclaimed, but she hung her head for a moment before looking back up with the usual fire in her eyes. "But it matters not. Mr. Wickham will not care, he loves me anyway. He told me so."

To get you into bed, of course he did, Elizabeth thought grimly. But she knew her sister, and this tactic would get nowhere now that Lydia had set her mind against it.

She turned to her proposed brother-in-law. "Will you do so, Mr. Wickham? Will you marry my sister, care and provide for her and any children you may have together? Will you be a proper husband to her? She is only fifteen, and will need you to guide her." *Right into drunken poverty laden with sin, I'm sure.* "Can you promise do so?"

He blanched briefly, either at the truth of Lydia's age or from the directness of Elizabeth's questions. Even Lydia was silent as they waited for his answer, though her face was cocky and triumphant where the other two were skeptical.

Then Wickham shrugged. "I'm not too keen on matrimony, and never ha' been," he slurred.

From the corner of her eye, Elizabeth noticed the corner of Mr. Darcy's mouth twitch. Mr. Wickham had certainly been keen to marry Miss Darcy, and on more than one occasion. She met his eye briefly and quirked an eyebrow in response. His mouth twitched again, this time into a ghost of a smile.

Mr. Wickham continued, unaware of the silent conversation taking place before him. "It wasn't my idea for Lyddie here to come along in the first place. That was all her, and I don't see why I should be punished for somethin' I didn't do. I don't have need for a bratty wife, nor any bratty babes, either."

"You said you wanted me to come!" Lydia burst out before Elizabeth could say anything. The triumph on her face had turned to angry disbelief. "You said I would make any journey ten times as fun, and you'd never met anyone you wanted to be with as much as me!"

Elizabeth held back the brutal truth that was on her lips—that Mr. Wickham would have said the same to any young woman who threw herself at him with no one there to protect her. "Lydia," she said calmly, "It may be that Mr. Wickham will see reason and remember his promises when he is more of himself. You cannot be married tonight, though, and you can't stay here. Come home to Aunt and Uncle Gardiner's with me and we can figure out your wedding details tomorrow."

Both Lydia and Mr. Wickham protested at that, Lydia asserting that she would not leave her dear Wickham, and Wickham claiming he would not marry. Ignoring them both, Lizzy stepped forward to gather her sister's clothes. The move put her within an arm's reach of Mr. Wickham, and in the next second, Elizabeth found herself grabbed roughly by the arm and pulled towards him.

CHAPTER THIRTEEN

Caught off guard, Elizabeth froze. The stench of Wickham's breath swept over her, clouding her nostrils with the scent of sweat mixed with cheap alcohol. "I don't want to marry your sister, but you'll do nicely," he said. "You're old enough to not whine like a babe, and smart enough to manage a household on whatever income we have. And I'd not mind taking care of your children, sweet, not at all. It would be worth it for the fun of making them!" he guffawed, then reached out his other hand to rub her back.

The world turned into a blur of motion, and when Lizzy could see clearly again she was in the middle of the hallway. Mr. Darcy stood between her and Mr. Wickham, holding the drunk man up against the wall by his neck.

"You will marry Miss *Lydia* Bennet," Mr. Darcy said. "You will do so, or I shall make life very unpleasant for you. Colonel Foster found a great deal of debts that you left behind in Meryton, a large number even for you. Does marriage really sound worse that the debtor's prison, or a one-way journey to America?"

"You'll never find me," Mr. Wickham rasped, struggling to speak through the hold that Darcy had on his throat.

Mr. Darcy dropped him roughly. "Perhaps not, but I'm sure you remember my cousin, Colonel Fitzwilliam. Go wherever you like, but he will sniff you out eventually, and make you suffer for all the time he put into looking."

"Would it not have been easier for us to become brothers, Darce?" Mr. Wickham asked, leaning himself back against the wall as if his legs could no longer support his full weight. Watching him, Elizabeth wondered just how much he'd had to drink. Surely a man of his habits could handle more liquor than the bottles on the table had contained.

"It certainly would have been easier if you'd been worthy of being my brother, George," Mr. Darcy responded with no feeling in his voice. "There was a time I would have been happy to call you 'brother.' You ruined that for yourself, not me." He looked up at Lydia, still standing frozen to a single spot in the room. "If you still want him, I will make sure he marries you. But your sister is right. You need to get dressed and come with us now. Your family is very worried about you."

Lydia stared at him, wide eyes blank, then seemed to catch herself. Moving slowly, she fumbled to find her dress and pulled it over her head sloppily, then hunted down her shoes and sat on the bed to pull them on. Lizzy guessed she'd had far less alcohol than Mr. Wickham, but it had obviously affected her as well, especially since she still drank watered-down wine at home.

"Ne'er thought I'd see you wi' Darcy," Mr. Wickham said to Elizabeth. "Didn't I tell ya wha' he's like? But ya sold out. Jus' like everyone allus does. He's too rish."

"I don't have to like Mr. Darcy to acknowledge when he is in the right," Elizabeth responded tartly. "He may be proud and little inclined to talk to those beneath him, but he has still been a gentleman today. You, sir, have not. Money has nothing to do with the matter. I wouldn't like Mr. Darcy for his money any more than I'd like you if you had ten thousand a year."

"But you do like me—or, yeh did," Wickham said. "I know it."

Darcy had moved into the room to help Lydia collect her few possessions, obviously thinking Mr. Wickham too drunk, or cowed, or both to do anything else foolish. So he was at least ten feet away when Wickham lunged at Elizabeth and yanked her too him. His mouth came down sloppily on hers and he pressed his body into hers against the opposite wall.

This time she didn't freeze. He'd left both of her hands free, and she shoved him away. Stronger though he was, she had the advantages of the wall braced at her back and a clear head. As Wickham stumbled back, Elizabeth delivered a resounding slap across his face. He snatched at her wrists, then froze.

Elizabeth hadn't seen a gun on Darcy once during the evening, but it was impossible to deny that he stood with pistol pressed against Wickham's temple.

"You wouldn't do it," Wickham whispered.

"Is that true?" Darcy pulled the hammer back with his thumb. "Why shouldn't I?"

Forcing herself to look away from the gun, Elizabeth caught sight of Lydia's face, completely drained of blood as she took in the scene unfolding in the hallway. Slipping behind Mr. Darcy, Lizzy crossed to her sister and gathered her in her arms, turning Lydia's face away from the men.

"Take us home, Mr. Darcy," she ordered in a tight voice.

He didn't look away from Wickham, his gaze as steady as his hand was on the gun.

"Now!" she snapped, glancing around the room to see if anything of Lydia's remained. A handkerchief lay on a chair—she snatched it up and returned to her protective position, then started to coax Lydia across the floor.

Finally, as the ladies reached the doorway, Mr. Darcy lowered the gun. "If you touch her, or my sister, ever again, I will kill you. I will burn in Hell for all eternity to keep you from hurting them."

Wickham sneered, but he was already stumbling. Grabbing him by the front collar of his shirt, Darcy threw him back into room and slammed the door behind him. They could hear him crashing into the bed and falling, curses and exclamations marking his fall. The closing door threw the hallway into near-darkness, and Lizzy was careful as she guided her sister down the hallway and stairs, wishing they could go faster but scared to run into something in the gloom. Mr. Darcy brought up the rear.

Finally, they reached the half-lit main room below, where Mrs. Younge waited with a scowl. Darcy pulled six guineas out of his pocket and showed them to her. "When Mr. Wickham wakes tomorrow, tell him I will await him at my club. I will make sure he is allowed entrance as long as he is fully dressed—I don't care how much he complains about his cravat. Do you think you can be bothered to remember that for an extra guinea?"

Mrs. Younge took her time considering, but at last she nodded. "Oh, I do believe I can, Mr. Darcy. It will save you coming back here and rubbing my face in my ruin, that's for sure. Have a good night sir, and a pox on your grave."

Mr. Darcy gave a short bow, handed her the money, and ushered Elizabeth and Lydia out into the night and the waiting carriage.

136

*

The ride back to the Gardiner's house was silent. Lydia seemed to be in shock and made no sound at all. She huddled around herself, and Elizabeth did her best to hold her sister as the carriage first bumped through rutted, narrow streets and then rolled down smoother, wider ones. Mr. Darcy stared out the window, his face an emotionless mask once again. The pistol had vanished from sight, but Elizabeth could not forget the sight of it— nor what Mr. Darcy had said.

I will burn in Hell for all eternity to keep you from hurting them.

They were not the words of a selfish man; she had known that immediately. How could she have once thought him cold, unfeeling, detached? He did not lack emotion, but felt deeply enough that casual conversation with strangers did not come easily to him—how could it? When she had occupied herself with witty comments and dancing, he had been worried for his sister. And she had judged him for it, laughed in his face about it—and then been the path that lead him back to deal with Mr. Wickham once again. How he must despise her now! Her sister could claim none of Miss Darcy's excuses. She had little prior connection, had thrown herself onto his mercy, had— well, Elizabeth would soon have to find out exactly what Lydia had done, or allowed to be done, but she knew better than to hope for the best. Not now, with Lydia starting to shake silently in her arms.

The carriage stopped in front of the Gardiner's house and between them Darcy and Lizzy bustled Lydia up the steps and in the front door without waiting for someone to answer a knock. The commotion drew a tired Mr. Gardiner from his study, and a moment later Mrs. Gardiner appeared behind him, looking equally exhausted.

"Lydia!" Mrs. Gardiner exclaimed. "We've been so worried for you. How could you run off like that? Where have you been?"

Elizabeth locked eyes with her aunt and looked upstairs, then down at her sister. They could ask and scold later—she had plenty of questions and admonishments planned already—but at the moment Lydia needed a bath and sleep.

Mrs. Gardiner nodded and turned to lead the way upstairs, stopping a maid on the way to request hot water for bathing. Lizzy nodded to her uncle, then followed her aunt, coaxing Lydia as if she was a marionette. She looked back once as they made their way to the upper stories, turning just in time to see Mr. Darcy and Mr. Gardiner walk into her uncle's study. The door shut, and she turned her attention back to her sister once again.

*

Nearly an hour later, Lydia was bathed and dressed in a spare nightgown. She had been sick twice, but did not utter a single word. Working together, Mrs. Gardiner and Elizabeth tucked her into Lizzy's bed. Lizzy readied herself for bed as well, then lay down beside her sister and snuggled in close.

Drained and stunned, Lydia fell into sleep quickly. Elizabeth, however, lay awake, staring at the ceiling and stroking her sister's long hair, replaying the night and wondering how they had ended up here.

*

Whatever had kept Lydia silent the night before was gone the next morning. Elizabeth had woken before her sister and slipped out of the bed, dressing and mentally preparing herself for a taxing day. She had not expected the stress to come in the form of Lydia's renewed exuberance.

Lizzy had just finished her breakfast when Lydia skipped into the room. "Is it not a fine morning?" she asked, sitting down and pulling a plate of toast towards herself and slathering a piece thickly with jam. "It is most fortunate that you found me, Lizzy, for I had thought I should have to do all the shopping for my wedding clothes alone, and not have anyone to help me carry the items."

Elizabeth and Mrs. Gardiner shared a disbelieving look.

"Did you not hear what Mr. Wickham said last night?" Elizabeth asked sharply. "He does not wish to marry you."

"Oh, la, Lizzy, you are so silly," Lydia said around a mouthful of toast. She poured herself a cup of chocolate, spilling some as she did so and ignoring it. She took a long drink, then went on, "Of course Mr. Wickham will marry me. He must, mustn't he?" Lydia gave a knowing, self-satisfied smile that told Lizzy exactly what she meant.

Dear Lord, she must marry him. There's no hope to save her other than that.

Lydia talked on through the rest of her meal about new clothes and a grand wedding breakfast, stopping now and then to mention how much she missed her dearest Mr. Wickham, and how much he must be longing for her as well. Elizabeth found herself glad she had finished her morning meal before Lydia's arrival, for she no longer had any appetite. Indeed, she was beginning to feel rather queasy as Lydia continued to speak.

As soon as she could, Lizzy excused herself and all but ran from the room, seeking the solace of her bedchamber. She had only been there long enough to begin a letter to Jane when Lydia entered as well, demanding that Lizzy reason with Mr. Gardiner,

"For he says I shall have no new dresses, or hats, or gloves, and no wedding breakfast at all! Lizzy, you *must* make him see reason!"

"Lydia, do you have no idea what you have done to our family?" Elizabeth burst out. "You have ruined all of us, and even if you marry your wretched Mr. Wickham, the rest of us will suffer. Mr. Bingley will not—"

"Oh, la, Lizzy, you are far too serious! Of course Mr. Wickham shall marry me, and of course you are not ruined. It was a lark, was it not?"

Lizzy picked up her letter and quill, quit the room, and went directly to her uncle's study.

As she had suspected, Mr. and Mrs. Gardiner were discussing their youngest niece when she tapped on the door and entered. Shaking her head in astonishment, Elizabeth addressed her uncle. "Sir, she will not see reason. She thinks it an amusing game, and I have little hope that she will change her mind. Lydia has always been notoriously stubborn, and will stick to her opinions as a matter of pride whether or not she is proven wrong. She has to marry him."

Mr. Gardiner sighed, rubbing a hand across his face. "You echo our own thoughts on the matter," he said tiredly. "The question is, can we make him marry her? Mr. Darcy believes that Mr. Wickham will demand money before he'll consent to marry her, far more money than Lydia's dowry will cover. Sadly, I agree with him."

"But he could be made to marry her?" Elizabeth asked, grasping onto that one strand of hope. "He will not disappear immediately?"

"Darcy believed that he would not," her uncle said. "He has dealt with Mr. Wickham before in—shall we say unsavory? —circumstances and believes he knows how the scoundrel will act."

Lizzy frowned at Mr. Darcy's continued assistance—and their nearly complete reliance on him. Aloud, she said only, "That is good news, then."

"We must keep Lydia here until matters can be decided," Mrs. Gardiner said. "If Mr. Wickham indeed disappears, we may be able to at least control the damage."

Elizabeth nodded. At any rate, keeping Lydia at home could not make matters worse. Letting her loose in London definitely could. She sighed. "Best lock the doors from the outside, then, and post a watch. Keeping Lydia contained may prove to be just as hard as locating her."

CHAPTER FOURTEEN

The following three days were agony for Elizabeth and Mrs. Gardiner. Tasked with keeping Lydia under control, they quickly devised a system for taking turns in her presence. Since Lydia could not be troubled to pay her young cousins any attention, let alone play with them, her presence was highly disruptive to the household and greatly unappreciated by the young Gardiners. As a result, Lizzie and Mrs. Gardiner traded off between Lydia and the Gardiner children—and the four Gardiners combined took less energy than Lydia did. Elizabeth never wanted to grab her cousins and shake sense into them, either.

At the end of a long morning filled with containing Lydia and amusing her cousins, Lizzy was all too happy to make her escape when the governess took charge of the children. *If only they could put Lydia back in the nursery,* Lizzy thought wistfully as she made her way slowly down the stairs to the first floor.

The door to Mr. Gardiner's study was closed, as it often had been since Lydia entered the house. Mr. Darcy had made several visits over the past days, but never at a time when Elizabeth was free to greet him—or thank him for saving her sister, ungrateful and infuriating as Lydia was. She made her way unconsciously towards the study now. If Mr. Darcy was there, she could finally thank him; if not, Mr. Gardiner might have an update on the situation with Mr. Wickham.

Of course, Elizabeth reflected, Mr. Darcy very well might not want her thanks. She wavered for a moment, then made up her mind and moved forward again. It likely wouldn't diminish his dislike of her and her family, but perhaps she would feel better if the words were said. She walked quietly down the hall, listening to see if voices came from the study.

They did. She hesitated, not sure if it would be appropriate to knock and interrupt during what must be a tense conversation already. While she waited, trying to make up her mind, she began to piece together bits of conversation as they filtered through the door. Full sentences escaped her, but she could tell one voice from another and make out phrases here and there.

Suddenly realizing she was eavesdropping, Elizabeth turned to go just as Mr. Darcy's voice cut across her uncle's, louder and more insistent than he had been before. "No," he said curtly, "I will not have you tell Elizabeth, and I certainly will not speak with her. I should not have involved her in the first place, and I will not further my mistake."

She froze, then hurried away, making for the solitude and sanctuary of the sitting room. He wished that she had not been involved. Perhaps if she had not been there he could have handled

Wickham—and Lydia—more effectively. Perhaps he would simply have paid Mrs. Young for information and passed it along to Mr. Gardiner, bypassing the need to see Mr. Wickham altogether. She had thought the pair of them had handled the evening effectively, though certainly not ideally. He must have an altogether different opinion.

The door to Mr. Gardiner's study opened just as she reached the sitting room, and she darted inside. She could not bear to see Mr. Darcy now, not when he had all but said that speaking to her further would be a mistake. Oh, she had been so blind to think he had changed from who he was at Netherfield. Dratted, prideful, insufferable man! Very well then, she did not want to speak with him either! How she wished she was at home, where she could escape the house and walk—

Elizabeth bolted upright. Surely her aunt and uncle would understand her need to go for a short walk to clear her mind before dinner. She made her way back into the hall—and found herself looking directly at Mr. Darcy, who had been coming towards the sitting room.

An awkward moment passed, in which she turned white and he, somewhat pink. Then he held out a letter. "My sister asked me to give you this, Miss Elizabeth."

She took it automatically. "Please thank her for me, Mr. Darcy.

There was an awkward pause. Elizabeth examined the back of the letter in her hands; Mr. Darcy shifted his weight back and forth between feet. Could he not even stand to be in her presence? Had the single sentence he'd been forced to say gone against his adamant wish of not speaking with her?

Very well then, she would not inconvenience him any longer than she already had. Elizabeth dropped a low curtsey and stepped back. "You must be anxious to return home, Mr. Darcy. I will not keep you any longer. Good day, sir." Without waiting for a response, she turned and escaped back into the sitting room, noting wryly as she went that the room had become quite the haven over the last few days. Making directly for her favorite chair near the window, Lizzy sat down and broke the seal on her letter.

Dear Miss Elizabeth,

I do hope you are still in London and this letter reaches you soon. I greatly enjoyed seeing you at Hyde Park last week and should like to continue our acquaintance if you are amenable to such a plan. Should you have returned to your home in Hertfordshire, perhaps we may establish a correspondence?

I fear I sound desperately needy, and would offer an excuse save for the fact that I have none. I can only say that I have few correspondents and fewer friends here in Town, and none of them understand the recent change in my emotions as you do. I do not mean to bother you, and please let me know if you are too busy for such a scheme.

I will sound needy yet again, for if you still remain in London I do hope you will join me for tea soon at Darcy House. I would love to visit you in Gracechurch Street, for I found your aunt most welcoming, but my brother will not allow me out into the city with sickness still present in some areas. Oh dear, it sounds dreadfully selfish of me to ask you to risk your health when I will not. Please do forgive me. It is just, I know William is overly protective and often takes precautions where none are truly needed. He has been quite distracted lately when he is home, and I do not want to worry him more than he already seems.

I shall end here. I ought to burn this letter and begin anew, but then I

*should only stare at the paper until I
rewrote all of the same things, and
you should never receive a single
word.*

Sincerely,

Georgiana Darcy

Elizabeth read the letter twice, delighting in its
contents. Georgiana's fresh voice was exactly the
distraction she needed to cheer her up. She
immediately made up her mind to call on her new
friend as soon Lydia's situation required less of her
attention. It would hardly be fair to leave her aunt
here to deal with Lydia and the Gardiner children
while she made social calls and drank tea in
Grosvenor Square.

Of course, it would be nearly impossible to visit
Miss Darcy at Darcy House without running the risk
of encountering *Mr.* Darcy. To refuse such an
invite from Georgiana, however, seemed nothing
short of cruel. Mr. Darcy could arrange to avoid her
for the entirety of the visit should he desire to avoid
her company. But she would wait until Lydia's
case had been settled.

*

Luckily for Elizabeth—and Georgiana—it was
only the next day that Mr. Gardiner announced that

148

an agreement had been reached. Mr. Wickham would marry Lydia by special license in two days' time.

While the news brought Elizabeth such relief as to move her to tears, it renewed Lydia's insistence on purchasing new clothes. When her pleas reached deaf ears, she then insisted that she and Mr. Wickham simply *must* travel to Longbourn following the wedding, to see her family before he departed to take up his new commission in the far north of England.

Elizabeth, listening dispassionately to her sister's demands, knew that Lydia was counting on Mrs. Bennet arguing in favor of a trousseau, or at very least the funds to purchase one upon arrival in her new home. Lizzy knew, as Lydia did not, that Mr. Bennet had been the one to order that no new clothes be purchased for his youngest daughter, not Mr. Gardiner. If her poor correspondent of a father had stirred himself to write and promptly send a letter with such instructions, Lizzy could only guess the force he had put into his orders at home.

The day of the wedding finally arrived. A note had been received from Longbourn just the evening before granting Lydia and her new husband permission to visit. Accordingly, Mr. and Mrs. Wickham would depart for Hertfordshire immediately after their wedding.

The news had brought Elizabeth a surprising amount of homesickness. No discussion had been had regarding her own return home, but it occurred to her that Mr. and Mrs. Gardiner might like their home to themselves, free of nieces. She would speak to Mr. Gardiner tomorrow about leaving Town. Today, he would have his hands full with her sister.

Elizabeth saw her sister off to the church with a great deal of mixed feelings. She was not to attend the wedding, and indeed had no desire to go. Her disappointment over what must be Lydia's future following her marriage would have been bad enough, but to put herself within reach of Mr. Wickham—sober or not, and she had her doubts— was not something she would voluntarily do again. So she stood on the front step and watched as her grim-faced aunt and uncle drove off for the church with Lydia bouncing exuberantly on the seat across from them.

The house felt empty after days of being filled with Lydia's exclamations and the stress she had brought. Elizabeth wandered into the sitting room and back out again, eventually making her way upstairs and to her room. She sat down at the small desk and looked at Georgiana's letter. Tomorrow, she would call at Darcy House to see her friend. Today, she owed Jane a letter with all of the last details of Lydia's stay—and then she would rest.

*

Darcy House looked just as imposing as it had during her previous visit, Elizabeth thought as she disembarked from the Gardiner's carriage the next day. It did not concern her nearly as much this time, however. She knew that the austere exterior turned into fine rooms filled with expensive items, but her thoughts were only on the inhabitants. Georgiana, she could not wait to see. If she was lucky, Mr. Darcy had decided a trip to his estate was imperative and had ridden off to Pemberley that morning.

The doorman let her in without question on this occasion, leading her silently to Georgiana's sitting room on the second floor. She flinched ever so slightly as they ascended the stairs, memories of Darcy's strong grip and stern gaze flooding back from her last visit. She was glad when they reached the top of the stairs and the doorman announced her presence to the ladies in the sitting room.

"Miss Elizabeth!" Georgiana exclaimed, rising as she entered and crossing the room to take Lizzy's hands in her own. "I am so glad you have come; I fear I have been subjecting Mrs. Annesley to far too many worries about staying home today rather than going to Hyde Park to sketch. Oh—" she remembered herself, "this is my companion, Mrs. Annesley. Mrs. Annesley, this is Miss Elizabeth Bennet."

Mrs. Annesley rose to greet Elizabeth, smiling. "I have heard much about you, Miss Bennet. I am pleased to make your acquaintance at last."

Lizzy returned the greeting, noting that the older woman seemed much like Mrs. Gardiner in bearing and temperament. She would have to suggest that Miss Darcy and her companion visit in Gracechurch Street once more before she left, for she dared not bring the wife of a tradesman to call on the pair in Grosvenor Square.

"Has Mr. Darcy decided it is safe for you to venture out into the city?" Elizabeth asked Georgiana as they all seated themselves. With Mr. Wickham gone from Town, she doubted that Darcy would continue to restrict his sister to her home. Well, Elizabeth couldn't blame his caution, not after witnessing Mr. Wickham's inexcusable behavior on more than one occasion.

"Yes," Georgiana responded, blithely unaware of Elizabeth's thoughts. "He accompanied me to Hyde Park yesterday afternoon, and that is the sketch I should like to return and finish. I was too excited at being out of doors at last to sit still for long."

"Surely you did not remain indoors for over a week!" Elizabeth exclaimed.

"No, I walked in our garden here at Darcy House," Georgiana acquiesced, "but it is not the same as going to the London parks."

"I understand your frustration," Lizzy said. "I am hardly myself when I have not had my walk for the day." Which had made it even harder to deal with Lydia while she stayed with the Gardiners—Lizzy had not managed to escape for a walk more than once. "What is your favorite thing to sketch?" she asked Georgiana, determined to not to dwell on her sister any longer.

Georgiana blushed slightly, looking away. "Well, I primarily sketch landscapes," she said. "Lately, though, I have been attempting to improve my portraits. I have few subjects, which makes it hard."

"Who do you draw?" Lizzy asked.

"My brother, Mrs. Annesley, my cousin and guardian Colonel Fitzwilliam—those I can sketch readily enough from memory." She turned redder. "I have tried a few of you, but cannot get your face right. There is something about your eyes that I have not been able to replicate."

"Would it help if I sat for you now?" Elizabeth asked, watching happily as Georgiana's face lit up with emotion.

"Really? You wouldn't mind?"

"Not at all. I should like to see a few of your sketches as well, if you do not mind. My sketching leaves much to be desired, but I do enjoy seeing other ladies' work. My cousin Julia is already far better than myself. She greatly enjoyed seeing you work when we met in Hyde Park, and has since exclaimed over several of the tips you showed her."

Positively glowing, Georgiana went to fetch her sketch book while Elizabeth and Mrs. Annesley chit chatted. They kept up the conversation as Miss Darcy settled in to sketch, although Elizabeth made an effort to keep her face still rather than letting her usual lively emotions show.

A pleasant quarter hour had passed in such a manner when the ladies heard the sounds of a carriage pulling up outside the house. Georgiana, who sat nearest to the window to utilize its light, looked up from her sketch. As her companion and Lizzy watched, Miss Darcy's already pale face drained of color and she turned to look at them with wide eyes. "I had best put this away," she said quietly, closing the book.

"Georgiana?" Elizabeth asked, unnerved and concerned for her friend. She and Mrs. Annesley both stood and moved closer to the teenage. "What is the matter? Who is here? Ought I to leave?"

Georgiana's voice was barely above a whisper, making it easy to hear the sounds of a loud, demanding voice downstairs. "It may be too late to leave, Miss Elizabeth. And our visitor is my Aunt Catherine, Lady de Bourgh."

CHAPTER FIFTEEN

Lady Catherine de Bourgh swept into the drawing room without waiting to be announced. She stopped several feet within the room, gaze fixed on Elizabeth. "You may greet me, Georgiana," she demanded without looking away.

"Good day, Lady Catherine," Georgiana whispered, though Lizzy doubted her words had carried across the room to where the formidable woman stood.

Lady Catherine sniffed, and finally broke eye contact with Elizabeth to turn. "Anne, you are tired from the journey. Sit on the chaise. Miss Jenkinson, make sure she has a blanket." The two other women, whom Elizabeth had scarcely noticed during her staring contest with Lady Catherine, scurried to do as they were told.

"Who are you?" Lady Catherine demanded of Elizabeth, turning back to fix her with a beady stare. "You are not one of Georgiana's school friends, or that awful grasping Bingley woman who came from trade."

Elizabeth glanced at Georgiana, who technically should have performed the introductions, but Miss Darcy was staring at the toes of her shoes. Elizabeth turned back to Lady Catherine and squared her shoulders. "I am Miss Elizabeth Bennet, your ladyship." She smiled politely and curtseyed. "I am a friend of Miss Darcy's, though not from school."

"Fah!" Lady Catherine exclaimed. "Friend to Miss Darcy indeed. You are nothing but a usurper, no better than that Caroline Bingley. You think to ensnare my nephew and become the next Mrs. Darcy, when such a privilege belongs to *my* daughter, Anne! Do you deny it?"

Elizabeth looked sideways at Anne de Bourgh, now swathed in a knitted blanket. The lady looked utterly uninterested in the conversation, and seemed to be staring rather fixedly at the ceiling.

"I do indeed deny such a plan," Elizabeth said firmly, meeting Lady Catherine's eyes. "I have no designs on Mr. Darcy, and would certainly never think to disrupt an established engagement even if I did."

Rather than being quieted, Lady Catherine turned red. "The engagement between them is of a peculiar kind. From their infancy, they have been intended for each other. It was the favorite wish of his mother, as well as mine. While in their cradles, we planned the union: and now, at the moment when the wishes of both sisters would be accomplished in their marriage, to be prevented by a young woman of inferior birth, of no importance in the world, and wholly unallied to the family! Do you pay no regard to the wishes of his friends? To his tacit engagement with Miss De Bourgh? Are you lost to every feeling of propriety and delicacy? Have you not heard me say that from his earliest hours he was destined for his cousin?"

Elizabeth was flabbergasted at the outburst, but even beyond that feeling was confusion. Where had this woman gotten the idea that she intended to marry Mr. Darcy?

"Your ladyship is quite mistaken," she said plainly. "I have never intended to marry your nephew, and I do not now. Should he desire to look for a wife other than his cousin, that is no business nor concern of mine."

"Have you no concern for your reputation, then? For his? Perhaps you simply have no care for yourself, being as lowborn as you are—yes, you see, I know your connections to trade! Your father's situation barely deserves to be called that of a gentleman! You cannot fool me, Miss Bennet! You and your family may have no concern for propriety or reputation, but I will not have my nephew tainted so!"

Elizabeth took a deep, steadying breath. Somehow this woman had found out about Lydia and Mr. Wickham, and Mr. Darcy's involvement in the matter. Was this how Darcy himself felt? If so, it was no wonder that he did not wish to speak with her. But as for the other comments, Lizzy was perplexed. Had Mr. Collins concocted a fanciful lie to save face after her abrupt removal to London?

"Your ladyship, I must confess confusion as to the rather harsh allegations you level at my family and myself. I am well aware of my family's situation and my uncle's livelihood, but do not see how that is any concern of yours. As for your more damaging accusations, I have no idea of what you speak."

"No idea! Are you simple, girl? You must be, to refuse a proposal from your cousin that would save your family from ruin, not to mention is most likely the only offer you shall ever receive! Very well then, I shall spell it out for you! You threw yourself on the mercy of your uncle to pursue my nephew, and have taken advantage of Georgiana's friendship to integrate yourself with the family and further your seduction!"

From the corner of her eye, Lizzy saw Georgiana and Mrs. Annesley both gasp in shock at Lady Catherine's words, but she had not finished.

"Your younger sister, thinking to follow in your example, threw herself at that dratted scoundrel son of the late Mr. Darcy's steward, who would not even marry her until your uncle paid him off! And from what Mr. Collins tells me, your elder sister is set to ensnare Darcy's friend in just the same way! Perhaps it will do for *him*, only one generation removed from trade, but I have come to ensure that you do not succeed in ensnaring my nephew! Even now I may be too late, but whatever has passed between you"—she sneered— "will mean nothing to him! A fallen woman can be disposed of, especially one like you. *He is meant for Anne!*"

For the first time she could remember, Elizabeth had no words of rebuttal, no witty way to turn the conversation and bring it back under her command, no way to save face. Lady Catherine's accusations were wild, some radically inaccurate—but all came just close enough to truth that Elizabeth struggled to find footing for a response, any response. To her utter annoyance, tears began to well up in her eyes. Oh, why must she cry now!

Keeping her face as emotionless as possible, even as she felt the first tear slid down one cheek, Elizabeth met Lady Catherine's gaze steadily. "My youngest sister has married Mr. Wickham yesterday. She acted inexcusably, as no young lady should, and she did so without encouragement or sanction from myself or from anyone else in my family. This is in no way your concern, as Lydia will now be wholly removed from any sphere of your influence."

Lady Catherine had turned a vivid shade of puce as she spoke, but Elizabeth continued.

"I have done nothing to warrant your censure, indeed I have never met you before today and doubt we will ever have reason meet again. You have insulted myself and everything I hold dear unpardonably, and for no reason I can discern. You can have nothing more to say to me, and I shall accordingly take my leave."

Lizzy turned towards a pale Georgiana, wishing she could reassure the young lady but knowing that a simple farewell was best at the moment. Before she could draw breath, however, Lady Catherine began a fresh rant.

"You lie! You fiend, you—you *whore*!"

The door crashed open, revealing Mr. Darcy. "*Enough*!" he bellowed. If Elizabeth thought she had seen him angry before, he now was furious. His face was red, and a vein pulsed on his forehead. He advanced into the room towards Lady Catherine, hands clenched into fists so tight his knuckles were white. "Desist, Aunt, or leave, I do not care which, but do so *now*!"

Lady Catherine's chin wobbled in outrage. "Really, Fitzwilliam, you cannot mean to tell me you have fallen under her spell! I am here to assist you—you cannot realize the mistake you are making!"

"Desist, I said!" he snapped. "I would silence you for the grave error of thinking you can come into my house and insult a guest, but I will throw you out for good if you push this matter further. I will not marry Anne and have never planned nor wanted to. Neither does she want to marry me, which as her mother you should already know! No, *you listen,*" he continued, voice raising over his aunt's as she attempted to protest. "I did not hear all of the accusations you leveled at Elizabeth, but understand this: if there is indeed a scandal linking our names, then I shall marry her at once and be happy to do so. We shall continue our acquaintance with you at her discretion, and you would do well to remember that!"

"For shame!" Lady Catherine yelled back. "Are the shades of Pemberley to be thus polluted! Oh, I am glad my dear sister did not to live to see this day!"

Elizabeth had slowly backed up as nephew and aunt battled in the middle of the room and now found herself standing in front of a door into the neighboring room. Thinking only of escaping long enough to compose herself, she seized hold of the handle and slipped into the next room, easing the heavy door closed behind her.

She found herself in the piano room, a light, airy room that was no doubt where Georgiana spend a good deal of time. Luckily, there were not only chairs but a window seat with curtains that could block the occupant from view of the room. Scrambling onto the seat, Elizabeth pulled her knees up and tugged at the curtains so they would shield her from anyone making a rudimentary inspection.

Elizabeth. He called me Elizabeth. The thought ran through her mind on repeat. *He said we would marry and he called me Elizabeth in front of everyone.* True, he had made the promise of marriage conditional, but Lady Catherine's ideas had to come from somewhere. Perhaps they had all been lies, concocted by Mr. Collins when Lizzy fled to London with the Darcys, but… *But what if they weren't?* And even if they were, truth would not matter if a scandal was already spreading. Anyone who had heard of Lydia's situation would be more likely than usual to think poorly of a second Bennet sister. Was she truly to be doomed to a life with Mr. Darcy?

Some time later, Elizabeth was recalled from her reverie by a commotion at the front steps. Lady Catherine hustled her daughter and Anne's companion into the waiting carriage and climbed in after them, her face still a magnificent shade of red that clashed with her burgundy dress. The carriage door slammed behind them and Elizabeth winced, feeling more than a little sympathy for Anne de Bourgh. Her own mother could be trying and embarrassing, but Elizabeth could not think of one occasion where she would have described Mrs. Bennet as vile, domineering, or cruel. In just one meeting with Lady Catherine de Bourgh, all words could be applied.

The main door to the music room opened and someone came in. Lizzy flinched. Maybe if she was lucky whoever it was wouldn't see her—but no, the footsteps crossed the room directly towards where she sat. Her only consolation was that the stride seemed calm and measured, not the quick, agitated steps of someone in a temper.

Mr. Darcy pulled back the curtain and looked down at her silently. His gaze was level, though she thought she detected a hint of pity as he took in her huddled form.

Elizabeth didn't want pity. "Do not fear, Mr. Darcy, you need not follow through on your promise to marry me. I do not know what Lady Catherine thinks I have done, but I would not be surprised to learn that my cousin Mr. Collins has fed her any number of lies at my expense to ease his wounded pride. If your aunt can be contained, then there is no reason for you to trap yourself in a," her mouth twisted, "most disadvantageous marriage."

"I am a man of my word, Miss Elizabeth. If this scandal is not of my aunt's invention, then I shall do whatever I can to shield you from it. If only to make amends for my aunt's most unjust words, I find myself quite interested in the matter."

She opened her mouth to ask his opinion on the source of the scandal, but what came out instead was, "You called me Elizabeth."

Darcy seemed caught off guard, and indeed Lizzy had surprised herself with her forwardness. "I did," he said after a pause. The corner of his mouth quirked up. "To be honest, it was likely what convinced my aunt I meant what I said about marrying you." His face sobered. "I am sorry for the impropriety. It was not intentionally done."

Elizabeth lifted one shoulder in a half-hearted shrug. "I suppose if we really must marry I had better accustom myself to the address." She paused. "Do you understand your aunt's accusations? I suppose we must begin by determining where she got her information—and what it is I am presumed to have done."

"Yes, that is the first step in my mind as well. In the meantime, you must be careful. It would not do to unwittingly make a rumor worse. I shall speak with my trusted servants when I leave you—they often hear news before I do, and may give me a place to start. I would ask—"

The door opened again and a tearful Georgiana crossed to the middle of the room, arms crossed. "How could you?" she burst out, glaring at both of them. "I am not a child, William! You kept me in the dark and refused to let me go out for fear of Mr. Wickham, not an illness! Do you really think me so naïve as to fall under his spell again? After what he's done!"

"Georgiana!" Mr. Darcy said sternly, but his hands reached out towards his younger sister as if to offer comfort. "I needed to know that you were safe. It was not what you would do, but what *he* might try that prompted me to keep you here.

When we found him—" he broke off and half glanced at Elizabeth, caught. "When I saw him only days ago he still spoke of marrying you. I did not want to test his desperation by giving him an opportunity to hurt you."

"So you *did* know; you were there!" Georgiana continued, turning her anger on Elizabeth. "How could you? You lied to me, both of you! And I thought you were the only ones I could really trust!"

She spun on one heel and marched out, slamming the door to the music room. Darcy moved to go after her, but Lizzy caught his sleeve. "Don't," she advised. "Let her cool down. She won't hear anything you say right now—it will all just be worthless excuses to her." She dropped her eyes, shoulders sagging, as she realized that once again this was her fault. "I am sorry. I asked you to keep the news of Lydia from her. This is my fault."

"No," Mr. Darcy said. "You asked only what would be expected in such a situation. This is my aunt's fault, and mine, as much as it is yours."

Elizabeth shook her head and untangled herself enough to stand, shaking out her skirts. "I fear that I will cause ruin to another part of your life if I remain any longer, Mr. Darcy. I bid you good day." She dropped a curtsey and walked out quickly, unable to meet his eyes, already feeling fresh tears begin to fall.

CHAPTER SIXTEEN

Elizabeth had thought to conceal her distress from her aunt and uncle, but no sooner had she entered the house on Gracechurch Street did her uncle call her into his study. His face was stern as she settled herself anxiously across from his desk.

"Elizabeth, I must ask you the meaning of this," he said quietly, handing over a page from the previous day's newspaper. She took it anxiously, noting with trepidation that it was from the gossip section. And there, halfway down the page, was the cause of Lady Catherine's visit.

Mr. Darcy of Pemberley in Derbyshire... seen furtively escorting a young lady after dark... lodging house of questionable repute... poor area of town... believed after further investigation to be Miss Elizabeth Bennet, daughter of a modest gentleman in Hertfordshire...

The section ended with a bawdy joke and a hope that Mr. Darcy could shield his impressionable sister from his questionable actions—and her. So this was the source of Lady Catherine's "information."

Lizzy looked up at her uncle, face burning in shame. He shook his head at her once, holding up his hand. "You went to help your sister. It was a noble idea, but no one will care about that—in fact, they will say you knowingly acted without regard to

167

propriety or reputation, and they would be correct. Handled incorrectly, this will also affect your sisters just as much as Lydia's predicament would have affected you."

Jane, was Elizabeth's immediate thought. Jane, who might still have a chance at winning Mr. Bingley's hand as well as his heart, could not be made to suffer because of her. She would have to accept Mr. Darcy's offer of marriage, and simply learn to live with it. To gain Georgiana as a sister would be a joy. Perhaps in time she would come to view Mr. Darcy as a friend. And as for love? Well, she just wouldn't think about love for now.

Her resolve in place, Elizabeth took a deep breath and began to tell her uncle what had taken place at Darcy House.

*

Darcy arrived for an interview with Mr. Gardiner early the next morning. A letter sat waiting and ready to be dispatched to Mr. Bennet once final details had been discussed, for his permission was still needed. Still, Elizabeth had little doubt that she would be a married woman in less than a month's time.

She had waited out most of the interview in the sitting room, alternating between pacing and sitting listlessly. Mrs. Gardiner kept her company for the wait, offering words of reassurance that left Lizzy

feeling less deserving by the minute. Since she had
rashly left Longbourn, almost everyone she knew
had suffered in some way, and Elizabeth could not
help but feel that the blame for a good deal of it lay
with her. Her family's name besmirched yet again,
Mr. Bingley perhaps driven away from Jane
forever, Charlotte Lucas shackled to a joke of a
man, her aunt and uncle obliged to trade their
peaceful existence to clean up after their nieces, and
Mr. Darcy and Georgiana forced to deal with a man
they both hated—and now to gain a wife and sister
they had not asked for. And how disappointed her
father must be.

"Elizabeth," Mr. Gardiner called out from down
the hall, and she sprang up from her latest seat.
Neither Mr. Darcy nor her uncle looked happy
when she entered, but Mr. Gardiner at least seemed
satisfied with the matter. Darcy's face was
unreadable, although Lizzy found that it no longer
bothered her as much. Her future husband was
predictable in his lack of expression, at least.

"Mr. Darcy has offered to marry you, Elizabeth,
and I see no reason to refuse him. Your father of
course will have the final say on the matter, but I
have written to him of my thoughts, and—" he
looked up at Mr. Darcy and raised an eyebrow—
"Mr. Darcy has included a letter for him as well. If
you have no objections, I will post the letter now."

I'm sorry, Papa. Elizabeth reached into her pocked and pulled out a letter of her own, postmarked to Jane but including instructions to show its contents to her father as well. "If you would post this at the same time, I would greatly appreciate it."

Mr. Gardiner nodded. He stood and added Lizzy's letter to the pile, then surveyed the two in front of him. "Mr. Darcy has also requested a chance to speak with you alone, Lizzy. I believe this is reasonable as well." He bowed his head to Mr. Darcy, fixed Elizabeth with a look she could not quite decipher, and then left, closing the door behind him with a finalistic *thud*.

"Would you care to sit?" Mr. Darcy asked after several long moments of silence had passed.

Elizabeth perched herself on the edge of a chair automatically, only to jump up again. "I believe I would do better to stand at the moment, sir," she replied, fixing her eyes on a knot in the wood of her uncle's desk.

Mr. Darcy stood, and she flinched involuntarily as he took a step towards her. "Elizabeth," he said softly, reaching out and taking both of her arms gently by the wrists. She had been twisting the material of her skirt without noticing. "You do not need to ruin your gown. I do not think I will be that bad of a husband, or at least I hope not to be."

"That may be so, but I cannot be the wife that you want," Elizabeth said, still not looking up. So much of what his aunt had said about her was true. How could he not resent her in time, even if he didn't now?

"I had not thought to take any wife, but that does not mean you will make a poor one," Mr. Darcy said. "And you will be a good sister to Georgiana. That is something I could not have found in any number of better connected young ladies."

Now she did look up, quirking one eyebrow without any of her usual humor. "You seem to forget that Miss Darcy is quite angry with me at the present. I will not be able to introduce her to anyone, or give her advice on fashions. It seems more likely that I will hinder Miss Darcy than help her."

"Georgiana will not want for lack of introductions, and there are always other avenues for fashion advice. What she needs most, and what you have already given her, is confidence and vivacity. As for her anger, she sent this for you." He retrieved a letter from his coat pocket and handed it to her.

Lizzy took it gingerly. "Does she know," she trailed off, unable to finish.

"She is aware of why I came here. I discovered the newspaper piece yesterday evening, and we had

171

a discussion of the day's events. I gave her an overview of our meeting with Mr. Wickham and stressed that you went only to help protect your sister. I believe she is sympathetic to your situation, having been through her own fear of scandal."

"I would not dream of comparing my situation to hers," Elizabeth replied stoutly.

"Nevertheless, her experiences have given her a far greater understanding of how an innocent or well-meant act can be taken in a wrong light and easily escalated."

Elizabeth nodded once, ceding the point.

"I have secured a special license for us to marry," Mr. Darcy told Elizabeth after a pause. "I—Elizabeth, do you have any requests for our marriage?"

She lifted her eyes back to his, completely unsure of what to say. "I—I had not considered the matter, honestly. I would ask that you allow me to see my family and—" she sighed. "I know this is not the marriage either of us had planned on, but I, I should like to feel like it is, well, real."

His eyebrows arched. "Real?"

Elizabeth turned away, examining her uncle's bookshelves. "If you marry me, Mr. Darcy, I ask that you do not act disappointed or angry with me simply for being myself on a daily basis. Of course, some of who and what I am must change as befits the mistress of Pemberley rather than a simple country girl. If you cannot take me for who I am and accept that, then leave me to my ruin."

She waited, clenching her hands in front of herself with nerves. He could take the offer, could walk away and ruin not only her but her sisters as well. Even for Jane, though, Lizzy could not consign herself to a man who openly regretted marrying her. Surely sweet, dear Jane would understand that, selfish as it was.

"Look at me, Elizabeth," Darcy said sternly, and she flinched. Here it came, the denial and rejection she had expected from the start. She took a moment to school her face into indifference before she turned.

He studied her for a long moment before saying any more. Finally, when she could hardly bear the silence, did he go on. "I would not have you change, not for myself or for anyone else. Do not think that this is all your fault. I could have gone after Mr. Wickham without you, or sent a man to fetch your uncle. I will not have you punished for my mistake."

But he would punish himself by marrying her. She could not see how he would feel any other way.

"Do you have any requests of me, sir?" Elizabeth asked quietly.

"You ask to see your family," Mr. Darcy began, and Lizzy's heart fell. He would ask her to avoid them, or visit without him. "I will never stop you from doing so, and I would welcome any of your sisters at Pemberley if you wish to invite them to stay, or your parents to visit. But I will not have Mr. Wickham in my home or near my sister."

Elizabeth looked up from her shoes in shock. That was all? "You forget, sir, that I have reason to avoid the man as well, and plan to do so as much as I may."

His face took on a dangerous look that she had seen the evening they found Lydia. "I have not forgotten, and I never shall."

She didn't know what to make of that, and so asked, "Do you have any other requests?" as much to change the subject as to gain information.

"I have two," he said after a pregnant pause.

It was her turn to raise her eyebrows in question, looking up from the floor to find him studying her intently. "Yes?"

"I would ask that you call me William, when you are comfortable with the idea," he said, turning ever so slightly pink. For some reason she was reminded of the first time he had heard her say the name, the way he had looked as she proclaimed to Georgiana that her cousin "William is my favorite." What had he thought that day? What was he thinking now?

"Alright," she said. "And the second?"

"Do not change, Elizabeth. No matter what some jealous lady like Miss Bingley says to you, stay who you are."

She nodded and smiled rather blandly and wondered how long it would take for him to change his mind.

*

They were married two days later before a small crowd. Mr. Bennet had sent his ready consent, but the family stayed in Hertfordshire. Mr. and Mrs. Gardiner came, as did Mr. Bingley and Darcy's cousin Colonel Fitzwilliam, on leave from his regiment for the occasion. Georgiana stood where Elizabeth had always assumed Jane would. At least Georgiana smiled shyly at her instead of scowling. As her letter had explained, she would have wished the same discretion from her sister, and could hardly blame her brother for keeping such a promise.

The ceremony was over quickly. Elizabeth's main memory of it later was Mr. Bingley's bright face congratulating them, and how hopeful he looked as he commented that "All the Bennet sisters seem to be marrying this season. Perhaps the whole family will follow suit by the end of the year?"

Mr. Darcy frowned at his friend's words, but Elizabeth took heart that Mr. Bingley had not entirely given up on Jane. How she wished that her sister could have been there! But Mr. Darcy had said that the sooner they wed, the less power the scandal would gain, and Mr. Gardiner had seconded his opinion. So Elizabeth said her vows without her beloved sister, realizing that even when they did meet again, she could never go back to being Lizzy Bennet. She must be Elizabeth Darcy now.

Mrs. Gardiner had arranged a small wedding breakfast, and Elizabeth greatly appreciated that her new husband did not seem to find the setting or the company beneath him—and that Caroline Bingley had not accompanied her brother. She, certainly, would have had unpleasant things to say about the house and family in Gracechurch Street.

Elizabeth was delighted by Colonel Fitzwilliam, finding him amiable where Darcy was stern, and full of anecdotes rather than taciturn. She noticed, however, an edge that suggested he could be just as severe as his cousin when the need arose.

All too soon, Darcy rose and looked at her expectantly. She swallowed down nerves and gave him a tight smile in acknowledgement. The plan was to depart London immediately for Pemberley, and if they were to make it to the inn where they would stay tonight, dallying was not an option. Elizabeth was not entirely sure how she felt about their imminent arrival and stay at the inn, but directly opposing her new husband's express wishes did not seem like a good start to their already uncertain marriage. Pushing back her chair, she stood as well and began to say her goodbyes.

CHAPTER SEVENTEEN

Someone had left a novel on the seat of the carriage. Elizabeth noticed it as soon as Mr. Darcy handed her in, but didn't dare touch it. Was it a trick? Had he put it there to test her obedience or strength of mind? There were many people, especially men, who thought novels were the devil's writing, temptation for young ladies. Did Mr. Darcy belong to that group?

He settled himself on the seat across from her and glanced at the book as well, then inclined his head towards it. "Georgiana thought you might like that. She often reads during the journey to Pemberley and back."

Perhaps it wasn't a novel. Lizzy couldn't imagine the strict Mr. Darcy allowing his impressionable younger sister to read one. She reached out and picked it up slowly, expecting to find a treatise on how to be more ladylike, but no, the book was indeed a novel. The author's name on the front page even read 'A Lady.' It had to be a trick.

"It will not bite you," Mr. Darcy told her, looking bemused. She looked up in surprise, and he continued, "You look at it as if it might turn into a snake. I thought you were fond of reading, but you do not have to read it if you would rather not."

"I do like to read, very much," Elizabeth said. "I must confess, though, that I have trouble believing you would approve of me reading a novel."

He looked surprised. "The thought of disapproving never occurred to me, at least not in your case. I was hesitant to let Georgiana read them at first, but she does not seem harmed by any of the ideas they present, and Mrs. Annesley monitors what she reads. This is one of Georgiana's favorites, or so she told me this morning when she left it here for you."

Of course, why should he mind what she read? He certainly had no reason to care about *her* as much as his sister. Still, Elizabeth couldn't help but feel touched by her new sister's care. "Favorite books are like old friends, don't you think?" she asked Mr. Darcy. The carriage lurched forward, and Lizzy leaned out the window, waving goodbye to her family. When would she see them again?

"I wouldn't know," Mr. Darcy said when they were both re-settled in the carriage. "I find that rereading books often bores me. I am far more interested in finding new information." He paused. "Of course, there are those books whose advice should be revisited from time to time, and I have gone back to revise opinions I formed in years past."

What a sensible, boring way to read, Elizabeth could not help but think. He must think her silly on

179

top of everything else, or perhaps she was exempt from serious reading as a female? But no, she could remember clearly what he had said that day at Netherfield when he had listed his requirements for an accomplished woman: *"...she must yet add something more substantial, in the improvement of her mind by extensive reading."* Well, she wasn't accomplished, not according to her husband. Resolutely deciding to not let his opinions interfere with her happiness, she opened the book and settled in to read.

*

The sun had set by the time they reached the inn. Elizabeth, who had let the carriage rock her into a doze for the last hour, stretched her arms out above her head and yawned as they came into the yard. Only when she opened her eyes fully did she remember that the seat across from her held her new husband, not Jane or Georgiana—and he was watching her, expression somewhere between surprised and amused.

Elizabeth colored, pulling her arms back into herself. She thought a side of his mouth quirked, but couldn't tell for sure. Wonderful. Mr. Darcy was laughing at her. Her mortification grew as he reached out to push an errant strand of hair back from her face. "Come," he said, opening the door and jumping out, then turning back to help her. "You must be exhausted."

Lizzy didn't know what to say. He seemed to find her entertaining at the moment, but perhaps that was because her lack of polish had been hidden from others by the carriage. Reluctantly, she followed her new husband out into the darkening yard. Elizabeth Bennet had never stayed at an inn—indeed, had never expected to stay in one— and so Elizabeth Darcy found it nearly overwhelming as servants hurried out of the inn to collect their items while yet another servant consulted the driver about the horses. The owner of the inn himself met them at the front door, bowing to Mr. Darcy before greeting him.

A few words, an exchange of money, and they were being shown upstairs to two adjoining rooms on the third floor. Following the innkeeper into the first room at Mr. Darcy's direction, Elizabeth found it plain, but clean. Her eyes went immediately to the basin and pitcher of water. How she should like to wash! She made up her mind to do so as soon as Mr. Darcy left.

The innkeeper showed Darcy the other room, which would be his, and then left them with another bow. Elizabeth had already started towards the wash basin when her husband re-entered her chamber.

"Where will the driver sleep?" Lizzy asked as the thought occurred to her.

"Downstairs," Darcy replied shortly. He frowned. "I should have asked, do you require a maid? You will have a personal maid once we reach Pemberley, of course, but I did not consider our nights on the road."

"No, I am fine, thank you." At home, she had always shared a maid with her sisters. The idea of having her own maid seemed foreign, no doubt the first of many such differences that she could expect.

He hesitated, and Elizabeth held her breath, sure that now he would offer his help to undress her—and then stay, as a new husband must undoubtedly expect to do. She could not refuse him, not after he had married her to save her from certain scandal, no matter how much the idea scared her.

There was a tap on the door, and a maid entered with a tray of food, which she placed on a small table. "Will ya be wantin' anythin' else?" she inquired.

Mr. Darcy looked at Elizabeth in question. She shook her head, and he turned back to the maid. "No, you may go."

The maid curtseyed and left them, and Lizzy's heart leapt back into her throat. She could not eat with the thought of what was to come after looming over her. Instead, she sipped at a cup of tea while her husband ate his fill of the meat and cheese. Finished, he stood and looked down at her. She did not find his unreadable expression amusing or reassuring now.

"It has been a long day," Mr. Darcy said after a pregnant pause. "I shall see you in the morning. Sleep well, Elizabeth." He went quietly to the door and left, closing it behind him.

Through her relief, Lizzy felt another emotion bubble up and grow, although she could not have named it if she tried. Here was proof that her husband truly did not want her, even in the basest sense that a man wanted a woman. Methodically removing her gown and petticoat so that only her shift remained, Elizabeth extinguished the candles and lay down.

The bed was cold and far too large for a single sleeper. The thought bit into Elizabeth. Certainly she did not want her husband to share her bed, but how she missed dear Jane! Tugging the blankets closer, Lizzy cocooned them around herself, wondering miserably if loneliness was to be her companion in her new life.

*

The next day passed similarly, although Elizabeth chanced a few remarks to Mr. Darcy. She was not made for silence or misery, and during the day felt some of her former high spirits return. Her husband answered her happily enough, but never started a conversation or said more than was required. He left her to sleep alone again that night, and in his departure she felt the isolation of the previous night crash back down around her. Distressed and unable to fully warm herself in the chill of the second inn, Elizabeth slept poorly.

She entered the carriage on the third day of their marriage expecting a similar display, and was quite surprised to find Mr. Darcy amiable and verbose. He spoke not about himself, but about the land that they passed through, and Lizzy realized they must be nearing Pemberley. His sentiment from the day she had first arrived in London came back to her, and she realized that the great Mr. Darcy must have missed his home as much as she currently missed Longbourn. The thought calmed her, and she found herself listening intently to his stories and asking questions to discern greater detail. The morning passed in companionable conversation, and Lizzy felt herself relax for the first time in the past three days.

Around noon Mr. Darcy announced that they were only fifteen minutes or so from the house, and Elizabeth looked out the window with renewed interest, full of curiosity about her new home. She had heard about Pemberley numerous times since meeting Mr. Darcy, but all of the comments simply seemed to boil down to one fact: it was a grand house with expensive furnishings in the midst of Derbyshire's beautiful landscape. Very few particulars had ever been given, and Lizzy did not have the faintest idea of what to expect from the house and surrounding park.

Mr. Darcy had quit speaking after making his announcement, and Elizabeth glanced over at him to find his gaze fixed on her. He looked almost expectant, an expression that changed to a slight frown as she watched.

What could have upset him now, when—oh. Pemberley had been much praised by Miss Bingley, and Mrs. Bennet had asked for particulars more than once. Mr. Darcy must expect that she should be rejoicing in gaining such a home, no matter what man came with it. Elizabeth sat back in her seat abruptly. Doubtless there were many young ladies who would think such a thing—Miss Bingley certainly seemed to be one—but she could not bear the idea that her new husband must think less of her in this situation as well. Clamping down hard on her curiosity, Elizabeth forced her attention away from the window.

"I forgot to ask you, will Georgiana be joining us soon? I recall she expressed a wish to spend more time in the country. Or will we return to Town for the season?"

"Is that what you wish?" His frown deepened.

"To return to London, or for Georgiana to join us at Pemberley? I must confess I have little desire to return to Town this year, for I have had far enough excitement, and—" she blushed— "it may be best for the scandal surrounding our marriage to die down somewhat before we return. As to the latter, I did think it would be nice for Georgiana to be able to join us, since it is her home as well. Of course, the decision is yours on either matter."

Several minutes passed in silence before Mr. Darcy replied. Lizzy found herself unable to keep from looking out the window altogether, though she did manage an impassive expression that she hoped spoke more of boredom than rampant curiosity. Oh, how beautiful the countryside was! How she should love to explore the paths and mounts, to see them without the impedance of a carriage window and the need to look uninterested!

But of course, she realized with a sinking feeling, Mrs. Darcy would surely not be allowed to roam freely across the countryside. The mistress of Pemberley was the grandest lady for miles in each direction, and would as such be expected to provide an example of proper behavior to those below her. At least, Lizzy thought wryly, there would be no need to run out in order to accept unwanted proposals here. No, that matter was settled without a doubt nor a choice, and it was settled permanently.

"I had thought," Mr. Darcy finally began, "to have Georgiana join us in perhaps a month's time. That way we are able to grow accustomed to each other in private. A marriage was necessary, but since it happened abruptly with little planning on either side, I hope to work through what differences we may have before my sister arrives. She is still quite impressionable and uncertain after her incidents with Mr. Wickham, and I want to provide her with a steady example of marriage not built off of false promises."

He surveyed her face, as if taking in her reaction to his words, and then continued, "I thought too that you may wish time to adjust to your new role as mistress of Pemberley without someone here who previously performed the duties of the role. The house is much larger than Longbourn, and the staff may be more open to accepting your authority if there is no alternative option."

Yes, the staff will know that I am a country girl not born to the role as Miss Darcy was. How kind of you to point that out, Mr. Darcy.

Elizabeth smiled. "That sounds like a well thought-out plan, Mr. Darcy. I shall look forward to Georgiana's arrival, and make what headway I can with the staff in the meantime." Surely they wouldn't all judge her—would they? Lost in thought, Elizabeth nearly missed the sharp turn that signaled their arrival at Pemberley. She steeled herself to keep up her uninterested façade, but worries over meeting the staff on their arrival held much of her attention for the remainder of the ride.

187

Then the carriage rolled to a stop and the door was opened by a waiting footman, throwing a waft of cold air into the carriage. Mr. Darcy jumped out, greeting the man by name, and turned back to offer her a hand. Oh, why couldn't he smile? Was it really so hard to provide some sort of reassurance?

Forcing back her unease, Elizabeth took the proffered hand in a grip that was slightly too tight as she stepped down—and stared. The house was at least five times larger than Longbourn! It was a large, handsome, stone building, backed by a ridge of high woody hills. Behind the carriage was a stream, gorgeous without any artificial enhancements. Having expected a pretentious home, Lizzy was blown away by Pemberley's natural beauty.

Mr. Darcy cleared his throat and she jerked her gaze to his face. "I would request the pleasure of accompanying you when you discover all of the walking trails which Pemberley has to offer," he said, a slight smile on his face. "I believe you may find them to your liking, but we shall have to defer that for another time." He inclined his head towards the door. "The staff are waiting to meet you and be introduced."

She took a deep breath, noticing that her hand still clutched his. Releasing it immediately, lest he think her immature or needy, she nodded once and tried for a smile. "I should be delighted to meet them."

Ready or not, she was home.

CHAPTER EIGHTEEN

Elizabeth had not dared to hope for her husband's continued absence at night, and so was not surprised when a quiet knock sounded on the door connecting their suites of rooms just after her maid had finished readying her for bed. Even if he did not want her enough to come to her at a traveling inn, the marriage would have to be consummated at some point, and didn't all men want an heir or two?

She didn't move from her spot by the fire or even look up, but Elizabeth was aware of her husband all the same. He closed the door behind him with a soft *click* and walked towards her slowly, stopping just as he came into the corner of her vision.

"Elizabeth." His voice sounded rougher than usual, and she wondered what he was thinking and feeling tonight. Likely not the awful uncertainty and nervousness that churned in her own belly, though what did she know?

"Mr. Darcy," she replied with far more presence of mind than she felt, not turning from the fire.

"Do you find your rooms suitable?" he asked.

She looked up, craning her neck slightly to see him. "Yes, thank you."

"If anything is not to your liking, or if you want to redecorate, you only have to mention it and it shall be done," he said, moving forward slightly so she could see him without looking over her shoulder.

"I thank you, but I am truly happy with them," Elizabeth assured him. "They are lovely, and I have quite simple tastes. The view from the window is all I would need for decoration."

"My mother was quite fond of the view," Mr. Darcy said. "I thought you may like it as well, considering your love of being outdoors. It gets quite cold here in the winter, as you experienced earlier today. This way you can enjoy the view when it is too cold to venture out."

His consideration touched her far more than she had expected, and she turned in her chair to smile at him. "I shall miss my daily walks, but Pemberley is so large I daresay I shall find plenty to explore indoors—assuming, of course, that you do not mind me doing so, Mr. Darcy."

"No, but to begin with it may be wise to take myself or Mrs. Reynolds with you. There are places in Pemberley where it is easy to get lost if you are not careful." Elizabeth had met Mrs. Reynolds, who had been housekeeper of Pemberley since Mr. Darcy had been four years old, earlier that day. She was an elderly, respectable-looking woman, and Elizabeth could not help but feel that they would have liked one another in different circumstances. As things stood, however, she had the distinct feeling that Mrs. Reynolds found her quite undeserving of Mr. Darcy, and could not imagine asking the woman for an intricate tour of Pemberley. Nor could she think Mr. Darcy would enjoy spending more time with her than necessary.

"I did not realize how long your hair is," Mr. Darcy said after a pause, surprising her. The maid—*her* new maid, Alice—had braided her hair for bed, which Elizabeth allowed and them promptly undid once Alice left for the night.

"Well, Mr. Darcy, since contrary to what some may think we have never found ourselves in a situation where my hair would have been down, I cannot express any surprise at that fact."

His mouth quirked up in a slight smile, and he took another step so he stood directly in front of her. He wore only breeches and an untucked shirt, and she opened her mouth to make a similar comment about never seeing him in such a state. Their eyes caught, and the words died on her lips.

"Elizabeth." It was just over a whisper.

"Yes, Mr. Darcy?"

"My name is William, Elizabeth. Perhaps you would call me that?"

Her mind flashed to her cousin, recalling his loud duck imitations and how he giggled when she rubbed her nose through his curly hair. Had anyone ever done that to Mr. Darcy, when he was a little boy called William?

"It is a much less proper name than how I am used to thinking of you," Lizzy responded, avoiding any actual use of the name.

"I can only imagine I look far less proper than you are accustomed to seeing me, as well," Mr. Darcy said. He was definitely smiling now.

Elizabeth blushed. "Yes," she said, unable to meet his eyes. In looking down, her eyes landed on his bare feet, and her blush deepened.

"That color is quite becoming on you," Mr. Darcy commented.

Elizabeth jerked her gaze back upwards, reaching out to smooth her dressing gown automatically in response.

"No," he said, smile growing. "Your cheeks."

"You mean to torment me with your teasing, Mr. Darcy," she said faintly, completely unsure of his motives. She did not imagine that he meant just what he said, but her confused mind struggled to understand why else he might make such a comment.

"I assure you I have no such goal. You are stalling, Elizabeth.

"I don't know what you mean," she lied.

"Then say my name."

"Mr. Darcy," she responded promptly.

He moved half a step closer so she had to tilt her head back to see him.

"Fitzwilliam," she said slowly, testing the feel of the name on her tongue. It was his full name, the one she had said once before when they pledged themselves to each other in the London church, but she would see why he preferred William. Fitzwilliam was such a mouthful, better suited for a family name, almost like—oh! Her curiosity won out over the uncertainty of the moment. "Are you named for your mother's family? Your cousin, Colonel Fitzwilliam—"

"His father was my mother's brother, yes," Mr. Darcy said. "And that is better, but not what I asked you to call me."

Oh, how she wanted to argue, to tease him, but she didn't dare. "William," she whispered, closing her eyes.

She felt him take another step closer and forced herself not to flinch or lean away. "Elizabeth," he murmured, reaching out one hand to touch her cheek. When she stayed still, he moved his hand back, combing it through her hair. She shivered, feeling goosebumps arise on her arms. "Are you cold?" Darcy asked.

Lizzy shook her head, but he had already bent down to take her hand and pulled her up from her chair. She stood stiffly, unsure of his intentions, and in fact he hesitated himself, dropping her hand. Somehow, that loss of contact only made her more aware of him, the heat that radiated off of his body only inches from hers.

His hand reached out, slipping beneath her dressing gown, and she gasped at the sensation.

"Elizabeth," he whispered again, turning and putting his other hand on her waist beneath her dressing gown as well.

His touch sent a wave of heat through her body that quite frankly scared her. She let out a ragged breath, trying to stay in control of her thoughts. Her aunt's words on the morning of her wedding came back to her, but now they made far more sense than they had in her sunny bedroom on Gracechurch Street.

"You will be nervous, but that is to be expected. Try to relax, and tell Mr. Darcy if you are uncomfortable. He has shown himself to be a gentleman; he will listen to you. It will be strange at first, especially since it is all new to you, but familiarity and ease will come with time. Some

*women enjoy their husband's visits as much as the
men do. You are brave, Lizzy, that will serve you
well."*

At the time, Elizabeth had felt that her aunt's
words were infuriatingly vague, but now she
wondered if such an experience *could* be put into
words with any true clarity. Could she explain such
sensations to Jane? Just thinking of trying caused
her cheeks to flame, and she ducked her head so Mr.
Darcy couldn't see and ask the reason. She couldn't
very well tell him she was thinking of telling her
sister about their, their—oh, there really *weren't*
words!

Her plan failed, for he moved one hand from her
waist to her face, cupping her cheek as he tilted her
face up. "Are you scared, Elizabeth?"

She stared up at him, trying to untangle her
thoughts into something that could be expressed.
"Scared, Mr. Darcy?" she managed, gathering a
shadow of her usual wit. "I will admit to some
uncertainty, for I am engaged in a dance that I have
never seen, much less been taught the steps."

A ghost of a smile crossed his face as he stared
down at her. "You have been doing well so far. I
sense you are a fast learner, and I will do my best to
be a patient teacher. I would not have you fear me,
or this, Elizabeth."

She looked away. "My aunt said as much," she whispered.

"Your aunt is a wise lady. Did she offer more wisdom?"

The color that had begun to fade rushed back. "She said it would take time to, to be comfortable."

"You're trembling, Elizabeth," he stated quietly.

"Yes," she told the floor.

"Look at me."

She looked up and he bent his head swiftly, touching his lips to hers. Before she could process what had happened, he pulled back and was watching her closely. "Was that so horrible?"

She blinked once, twice, working through the mishmash of emotions clouding her mind. "No, sir."

"I thought you were calling me William," he murmured, bending his head again to hers. This time there was nothing swift about the kiss. He left one hand on her cheek, pulling her tight against him with the other arm.

Sensations ran like wildfire through her body. How could she possibly feel so hot and cold all at once? And how could his embrace feel so foreign and yet so natural? She gasped against his lips even as she began to relax into his hold automatically.

His hand left her cheek and pushed the dressing gown off her shoulders so it fell into a puddle at her feet, then returned to tangle in her hair. Was this how it felt to be weak at the knees? Lizzy Bennet had always scoffed at such an expression, proud that her own knees had never failed her. Now, though, she brought her hands up to brace them on Darcy's shoulders, glad his grip kept her from simply sliding to the floor. When he finally broke the kiss, both of them were panting.

"Was that so bad?" he whispered into her hair.

She made a strangled sound in response, and he pulled back, tipping her face up to see her expression. Finding no tears or other signs of trauma, he chuckled slightly. "Do you trust that I won't hurt you, at least not any more than I have to?"

Her aunt had made a vague mention of pain as well, so while the phrasing concerned Elizabeth, she did not find it altogether unexpected. "Yes," she said without reservation, surprising herself. She *did* trust him. He may not have wanted her as a wife, or even like her, but his every action inspired trust. It was almost laughable that she had once thought Mr. Wickham the more honorable man!

Mr. Darcy kissed her again, just as intensely as before, and this time her knees did give way. He swept her up as if she weighted no more than a child and carried her the short distance to the bed.

Rather than lay her down as she expected, though, he sat on the bed and settled her so that she sat firmly on his lap.

The position was another completely new experience. She had been carried once or twice in memory, having injured her ankle in several impulsive actions throughout the years, but never had someone held her like a child would hold a favorite doll. Even through the strangeness of the sensation, she felt protected.

Then he was kissing her again, running hands through her hair and up her back but somehow managing to maintain a firm hold on her all the while. Slowly, she brought the hand not trapped against his body up to his chest, running it lightly up to his shoulder and tracing the seam of his shirt partway down his arm. He groaned in response and pulled her closer, one hand firmly gripping her backside as he moved her, the other still tangled in her hair.

"Elizabeth," he whispered against her lips, voice reverent. Suddenly she was lifted again as he stood and laid her down on the bed. He stepped back to strip off his shirt and she had just enough time to notice the chill of the room before he had rejoined her, sending heat of more than one type coursing through her veins.

She sucked in a breath as his hand slipped beneath the hem of her nightgown and trailed up one leg. Freezing in place, he looked up and met her eyes. "Are you scared, Elizabeth?"

Yes! the rational part of her brain screamed. But she wasn't thinking with the rational part of her mind—didn't know if she was thinking at all—and heedless feeling that had proceeded every major scrape she had ever gotten herself into was taking over, burning away her concerns and resistance. The question gave her pause, and for a moment she wavered on the edge of the precipice between everything she had ever known and the new sensations threatening to overwhelm her.

"You are brave, Lizzy, that will serve you well."

"No," she whispered, pitching herself forward into the unknown with only his hands to guide her, knowing as she fell that the girl she had once been existed no more.

Chapter Nineteen

Elizabeth woke early the next day wondering if the previous night had been a dream. But no, she was slightly sore and there was her dressing gown on the ground before the fire, which had burned down to embers. Mr. Darcy had been right, Elizabeth thought as she burrowed down farther into her covers. Derbyshire was cold.

The movement caused the pain between her legs to increase momentarily, and she buried her face in the coverlet as though that could block out the memories of what had caused the discomfort. At least Mr. Darcy—*William*—had not stayed with her. Oh, how she had wanted him to last night, for the second he stopped touching her she had felt all the confusion and uncertainty over what they had done.

Of course, she could have asked him to stay and he likely would have complied, but she would not beg for affection, and how could she face him now? In the light of day, it was clear to her just how awkward this morning could have been. No, better that he come and go in the dark. Wondering how she would manage to face her husband when they did eventually meet that day, Elizabeth fell back into a restless sleep.

*

When Elizabeth awoke next, the fire was blazing and light streamed in through a slit in the curtains.

"Good morning, ma'am," Alice said, turning to face Elizabeth once she had placed her pitcher of water next to the washbasin.

A quick glance told Elizabeth that her dressing gown had been moved from in front of the fire. Did the maid know what it meant, or would she assume her new mistress was a slob with little care for her clothing? A moment later, Lizzy realized she didn't know which option she preferred. At least her husband's attentions were natural, or so she assumed.

"Good morning, Alice," Elizabeth responded. Too long had passed since the maid's greeting, but better to be slow than altogether rude, Elizabeth decided. She sat up, wincing slightly, and swung her legs over the edge of the bed.

The sight of blood on the sheets stopped her cold. She had washed herself last night, after, but in the dark had given no thought to the bed. Standing quickly, she tossed the coverlet back over the incriminating stain.

Alice must have noticed her unease, because she smiled. "I have a pitcher of warm water ready for you, ma'am. Don't worry about the bed, I'll see to it later."

Elizabeth stood frozen, feeling her cheeks heat.

The maid stopped what she was doing and came to stand before Elizabeth. "Mrs. Darcy, this may be improper of me to say, but truly do not worry yourself. I was in the employ of another newly married lady before leaving London, and I am accustomed to the, well, difference in needs between yourself and unmarried girls. Everything will be taken care of."

She bobbed a slight curtsey, looking slightly worried at having said too much, and went back to readying Elizabeth's clothes for the day.

"Alice," Elizabeth said.

"Yes?" The maid turned back to look inquiringly at her.

"Thank you."

Alice smiled again. "At your service, ma'am. Now, what would you like to wear for the day?"

*

Elizabeth only got lost once on the way to the breakfast room, which she considered a small victory. Mr. Darcy had given her a brief tour of the main rooms upon their arrival the day before, she knew immediately that getting lost would be inevitable. The rooms themselves were not too hard to remember. It was getting between them that proved to be the problem. How she would ever feel at home in the sprawling house was a mystery to Elizabeth, one she tried her best to forget as she exited her room and made her first solo attempt at navigating the hallways of Pemberley.

The room was empty when she entered, but a maid followed close on her heels, carrying a tray with toast, jam, and a tea pot. "Good morning, ma'am," the girl said, bobbing a small curtesy before placing her burden on the sideboard. "Will you be having tea this morning?"

"Yes, please," Elizabeth said, eyeing the setup of the room. She had hoped to find her husband here, if only so that she could mimic his actions. In his absence, she was left with the options of potentially making a faux pas or asking a servant what was expected of her—and both would give the staff reason to ridicule her should the maid repeat what she had seen and heard.

About to open her mouth to ask—and bear the consequences as she must—Elizabeth spotted a small stack of plates at one end of the sideboard. Relieved, she took one and chose a piece of toast while the maid poured her tea and placed it at the table.

"Has Mr. Darcy already breakfasted?" Lizzy asked as she took a seat, trying for a casual tone and hoping that the question did not convey anything unsavory. What was the protocol for this situation? Oh, if only Georgiana had arrived with them!

"Yes, ma'am," the maid said, her face giving no clue to whether or not Elizabeth had made a mistake in asking. "The master is a very early riser. I believe he has already ridden out to examine the estate. He asked that your maid tell the kitchen when you were ready for breakfast. Will you be needing anything else?"

"No, thank you," Elizabeth said, considering what she had learned. Lost in thought, she hardly noticed when the maid curtseyed again and left the room.

Elizabeth finished her toast without tasting it, then stood and walked over to the window with her tea. Gazing out over the well-manicured lawn and the wilder but no less impressive landscape beyond, she wondered exactly where her husband might be at the moment and when he might return. It was natural, of course, that he should be anxious to see his estate after a long absence. Indeed, there was no reason for her to feel temporarily abandoned, cast off as a burden he did not wish to deal with just now. No reason at all.

Well, there would be no option but to ask Mrs. Reynolds for the extended tour of Pemberley. She would not wander about her new home like a visitor while waiting for Mr. Darcy to find time for her. If luck was on her side, perhaps spending more time with Mrs. Reynolds would improve the housekeeper's opinion of her.

Resolved, Elizabeth finished her tea and turned to exit the room before she noticed the next flaw in her plan—she did not know where Mrs. Reynolds could be found, nor what protocol should be followed to contact her. At home—at *Longbourn*, she corrected herself—she would start any search for Mrs. Hill in the kitchens. Of course, the kitchens were very likely the best place to begin locating Mrs. Reynolds as well, but Elizabeth highly doubted that her presence would be welcomed below stairs at Pemberley. Of the possible faux pas she could make her very first day as mistress, that one topped the list.

After several moment's consideration, Elizabeth placed her tea cup on the table and left the breakfast room, making her way sedately down the hall. She paused to examine portraits on the walls and surreptitiously checked the rooms that she passed, finding a music room and formal drawing room before discovering what appeared to be the less formal morning room. She entered and made her way immediately across the room to the high windows. These looked out over the back of the house, showing a large garden that Lizzy thought would be splendid for walking when the weather finally turned warmer.

She turned her attention to the room itself, pleased to find an elegant writing desk set where one could make the most of the natural light from the windows. A neat stack of paper, stoppered bottle of ink, and several quills were inside. Soon she would come write a letter to Jane, and another to her Aunt Gardiner, Elizabeth thought as she closed the lid of the desk and resumed her inspection.

The rest of the furniture, though far finer than that in Longbourn's sitting room, proved to be both comfortable and well-used. Lizzy found one chair in particular, set to just one side of the fire, which would be perfect for reading during the cold winter months when the only adventures she could expect would be those on the printed page.

Lost in contemplation, Elizabeth almost missed the footsteps on the carpet behind her. Turning to find Mrs. Reynolds, she barely caught herself before she curtseyed to the woman. Hoping to cover her moment's confusion, she smiled. "Good morning," she said pleasantly, hoping her tone didn't come off as too familiar.

Mrs. Reynolds gave a short curtsey that seemed to be more a bob of her head. "Good morning miss—excuse me, Mrs. Darcy." Her expression was agreeable, but she did not smile. "I came to see if you would be interested in a tour of Pemberley this morning, but I see you have found some of it already."

Elizabeth felt herself flush, as if she should had trespassed into the sitting room. "Yes, Mr. Darcy gave me a brief tour yesterday, so that I should not feel too lost when I ventured out of my rooms. He had mentioned taking me on a longer tour today, but I understand that he is currently busy with estate matters. I would be delighted to go with you instead, for I am most interested in making myself acquainted with my new home."

Lizzy forced herself to stop, realizing that she was babbling. Continue talking, and she was sure to dig herself into a hole—it would not do to talk about Pemberley's splendor too much lest Mrs. Reynolds think her only interested in money. Similarly, she knew better than to apologize for taking up too much of the housekeeper's time, but that had not stopped the comment from forming on the tip of her tongue at least twice.

From the less than impressed expression on Mrs. Reynold's face, she was aware of Lizzy's nervousness. Of course, a lady born and raised in such a house as Pemberley would not find it, nor its housekeeper, intimidating in the slightest. Elizabeth had enough presence of mind to realize that if her circumstances were different—say, if her husband had married her for some reason other than to mitigate a scandal—she would likely feel confident and happy to explore Pemberley and meet the staff. As it was, Elizabeth did her best to keep her chin up and a smile on her face as Mrs. Reynolds, who had begun talking without Elizabeth retaining any of her words, led her out into the hallway to begin the tour.

"I suppose you'll be wanting to start with the grand rooms on the ground floor," Mrs. Reynolds commented over her shoulder as she headed towards the staircase.

The words made Lizzy frown, but here was a chance to improve the housekeeper's opinion of her, if handled correctly. "No," she said, stopping short.

Surprised, Mrs. Reynolds turned and raised her eyebrows. "No?"

"By all means, let us begin on the ground floor if you think that is the most logical stop, but I do not wish to see Pemberley as if I am a visitor, appealing to the housekeeper," she inclined her head slightly, "for the tour so that I may be impressed. If I am to be mistress of Pemberley, then I mean to be mistress of the whole place, not just the rooms meant for display."

Mrs. Reynolds studied her in silence for several moments while Elizabeth held her breath. Finally, she said, "I see. Well, then, Mrs. Darcy, I will take you at your word. We may as well start here, work our way around the courtyard, and then go back to the ground floor. And while you may not look to be impressed, I will find you a fool if Pemberley doesn't impress you anyway."

She turned to the nearest room and Elizabeth was left to catch up, turning the housekeeper's blunt words through her mind and trying to determine if any progress had been made.

They toured the ground, first, and second floors, and Elizabeth was more often than not rendered speechless by the fineness of her new home. *Mrs. Reynolds needn't think me a fool, no matter what else she* does *think,* Elizabeth thought as she stared in aww yet again, this time at the chapel. They had visited bedrooms and dressing rooms, both for guests and family members; dining rooms of different formalities; sitting rooms; a ballroom; an armory; the library, even more wondrous than Elizabeth could have imagined; and several galleries.

The hallways themselves were magnificent with their paintings and the ever present grand views from the windows, and the staircases were works of art. Elizabeth had found Darcy House in London to be the finest residence she had ever seen, but next to Pemberley's magnificence it may as well have been Longbourn. And of all this she was mistress!

They ventured briefly into Pemberley's courtyard in the center of the house, and somehow it was this view that allowed Elizabeth to understand how the wings of the house were oriented—and why there had been so many turns when she was looking for the breakfast room that morning. She by no means felt confident in navigating between the many rooms, but Elizabeth had gained a great deal of understanding from Mrs. Reynolds' comments on each room. The rest, she supposed, would come with time.

CHAPTER TWENTY

Mrs. Reynolds had offered, somewhat halfheartedly, to show Elizabeth the stables when the latter expressed her interest in the place. Luckily for the housekeeper, they exited the house just as Mr. Darcy was riding past. He stopped his horse at once and swung down, leading his mount over to where the women stood.

"Good morning, Mrs. Darcy, Mrs. Reynolds," he said formally, coming to a halt in front of them. The horse, looking sweaty and well-ridden, seemed content to stand just behind Darcy's shoulder.

Elizabeth gave a small curtsey and couldn't resist smiling up at her husband mischievously. "Good afternoon, sir."

She immediately hoped the words would not be taken as disrespect, but Mr. Darcy simply looked up and gaged the position of the sun. "I daresay you're correct, Elizabeth," he commented. "And did you have a pleasant morning?"

"I did. Mrs. Reynolds was kind enough to show me a great deal more of the house—in fact, so much of it that I'll likely need another tour just to recall which rooms were which."

To her side, Mrs. Reynolds snorted slightly, but Mr. Darcy simply raised one eyebrow. "And what did you think of the house?"

"Splendid, sir. I've no need to ever visit the palace now, for I would certainly be disappointed."

He smiled, a real smile that touched her. "I shall keep that in mind should an invitation come from Prince George."

Absorbed with the realization that such an invitation very well might come for the great Mr. Darcy, Elizabeth missed the beginning of Mrs. Reynolds comment.

"—the stables, sir. Perhaps you would like to show her yourself? No doubt the new maids have turned my kitchen on its head by now."

Mr. Darcy chuckled. "Go save your kitchen, Mrs. Reynolds. I'll be happy to show Mrs. Darcy the stables, and anywhere else she has yet to see."

"Thank you so much for the tour," Elizabeth said. Mrs. Reynolds gave her a courteous nod—an improvement, if a small one—and left them, hurrying back into the house.

"Did you have a good ride?" Lizzy asked.

Mr. Darcy turned and began walking up the hill to the stables, motioning for her to join him. "I did. There are a few places I was most anxious to review. The men will have several projects waiting for them when the ground thaws this spring." They walked several paces. "And how did you find Mrs. Reynolds?"

"Very knowledgeable," Elizabeth answered honestly.

"She has been with the household since I was a young boy. I cannot recall Pemberley without Mrs. Reynolds."

"She seems very fond of you," Lizzy remarked. The housekeeper had made that fact abundantly clear throughout their tour, all the while maintaining an air that conveyed her assumption that Elizabeth disagreed and insinuating that she was most definitely not good enough for him. Once again, Elizabeth thought she would have laughed, had her own confidence in her situation been higher.

"She is fond of reminding me that she patched me up after many of my less advisable escapades as a child. I can never be the grand master around Mrs. Reynolds."

How Elizabeth longed to confide in her husband that the housekeeper treated *her* with poorly concealed disdain, but she bit her tongue. He had not asked to have her here, and her pride would not allow her to create more strife in his household than she had undoubtedly done already. Surely Mrs. Reynolds would come to like her more—or at very least, dislike her less—in time.

They had nearly reached the stables by this point, and an old white dog trotted slowly out, wagging his tail as they closed the remaining distance. A stable hand followed him out, coming over to Mr. Darcy to take his horse's reins. Darcy relinquished them with his thanks and a pat on the horse's hindquarters as they passed. The pair vanished into the stables, and Mr. Darcy turned his attention to the dog.

"Elizabeth, let me introduce Orion," he said, getting down on one knee to pet the dog, who leaned into him affectionately. "Orion is one of the best hunting dogs I've ever had, and he still makes for a good companion."

Elizabeth started to kneel as well, then remembered that sending stained and soiled dresses to the maids would not be the way to win their affection—or to convince them she was worthy of her new position. She settled for bending, offering her hand for the old dog to smell and then scratching him behind the ears. His tail wagged faster, and he turned to lick her arm.

"He's a wonderful dog," Lizzy said, giving an involuntary shiver as she spoke.

Immediately, Darcy stood. "You're cold. Come, it will be warmer inside." He ushered her into the stables, which were indeed warmer than the chilly Derbyshire air.

Elizabeth had never been inside what she considered to be a proper stable before. Her father kept a few horses, but they were used for working on Longbourn's farm and occasionally pulling their carriage. Only rarely did the Bennets ride, and Lizzy had long since fallen out of practice.

Even to her untrained eyes, the horses in the Pemberley stable were gorgeous. Their manes were well-combed and their coats gleamed. Many of the horses were chestnut, similarly colored to the stallion that Mr. Darcy had been riding, but Elizabeth saw a black horse and several greys as well.

Darcy motioned towards the black. "This is my usual mount, Excalibur. He's the grandson of the last horse my grandfather ever purchased."

For some reason, the words made Elizabeth pause. What would it be like to have a place that was so securely *yours*? No entail, no question that you belonged here—that this was a place made by your ancestors, for you. Mr. Collins had long existed only in Mrs. Bennet's worries, but Elizabeth couldn't remember a time when she hadn't known that he did indeed exist.

"Do you ride often, Mr. Darcy?" she asked to cover the pause that had already gone on too long.

"I do," he responded. "When I am home I ride nearly every day, to check on the estate and test new horses in the stables. You said once that you do not ride, I recall. Do you not like it, or did you simply never learn?"

216

"Some of both," she replied honestly. "We didn't have any horses kept just for riding, and so I never practiced enough to be comfortable. It has been years since I rode last."

They stopped in front of a stall containing a small chestnut mare. "This is Sundance," Mr. Darcy said. "I thought that she may be a good fit for you, especially since I assumed you had not spent much time on horseback. It is the best way to explore the estate and the countryside." He looked down at her and she thought she detected a hint of a smile. "You may even like it as much as walking, once you are more accustomed to riding, and Sundance will always be available for you."

"As much as walking, sir? Surely not," Elizabeth replied. The idea of having a horse just for her use was alien to her. She had never even considered such a thing—Lizzy Bennet had little thought for horses. Still, she reached out a tentative hand to stroke Sundance's soft nose.

"Perhaps not, but riding is far better suited to the mistress of a large estate," Mr. Darcy said. He pulled a sugar cube from a pocket in his jacket. "Here." He took her hand and gently moved her fingers so they were all pressed together and flat, then placed the sugar cube on her palm. "Give her this."

Elizabeth held out her hand to the mare, who took the cube daintily, her whiskers tickling

Elizabeth's hand. She giggled softly at the feeling, but her heart had sunk at Mr. Darcy's comment, and much of the joy was removed from the moment. The horse was no longer just a gift, but a tool to help compensate for her current lack of skill and sophistication.

They finished the tour of the stables, and while Lizzy made exclamations of delight and expressions of interest when required, they required effort that genuine feelings never did. Finally, for Mr. Darcy had conducted a most thorough tour of the stables and the small kennel attached to them, they exited into the chilly air to return to the house.

Orion trotted over and walked between them as they made their way down the lane. "Is he allowed inside?" Elizabeth asked, reaching out to scratch his head. The dog was tall enough, and she short enough, that she only needed to stoop slightly to reach his head.

Assuming that no creature would be allowed to sully Pemberley's immaculate interior, Elizabeth was surprised when Mr. Darcy responded, "Oh yes, he comes in quite often. Mrs. Reynolds will have my hide if I don't check his paws for mud, but he's a pleasant companion for reading or writing letters. Did you have dogs at Longbourn, Elizabeth?"

"Several," she replied. "They were generally kept outside, though. My mother refused to allow them in her sitting room, and since none of them were ever fully trained I cannot blame her. They were not hunting dogs, you see, just farm animals," she added, fully aware that she had just underscored another difference in her upbringing, but determined not to give a false impression.

"That is understandable," Mr. Darcy said as they climbed the front steps. "It takes a good deal of time to train a dog correctly, at least for hunting, and your father does not seem the type to hunt when he could simply read about the sport from the comfort of his library."

"You are correct, sir, it interests him little," Elizabeth said, wondering if this was yet another deficiency in her background. Surely not all rich gentlemen hunted—she would laugh aloud to see Mr. Hurst on the back of a hunter, his bulk stuffed into a hunting costume.

They had entered the house and were in the middle of the grand entrance hall. Mr. Darcy stopped abruptly and turned to Elizabeth. "What happened to calling me William?" he asked quietly, looking down at her.

Not prepared for him to stop, she had come to a halt just behind him. Looking directly up at her husband, she was reminded strongly of the scene on the stairs of Darcy House in London and felt her cheeks heat. Then her mind processed his question and she colored more. "I—" she looked away and tried again. "I thought that perhaps, well, that you meant," she stopped and dropped her eyes to the ground, certain that her face must be a brilliant shade of crimson.

"That I meant you were only to call me that in private?" he asked, voice completely neutral.

"Yes," she told the glistening marble of the floor.

"Does it bother you when I call you Elizabeth?"

She frowned, not having considered his question before. He gestured towards the stairs, and they walked on. "No," she said slowly. "Perhaps because it is so close to what you called me before, it does not seem so strange. It is far more strange to be addressed as Mrs. Darcy, to be honest." She chanced a look up at him and found his eyes on her. "If I recall correctly, you called me Elizabeth before we were even engaged, sir—William."

He gave a small smile. "I believe I did, Elizabeth. If we are being honest, then I confess that I thought of you as Elizabeth for some time."

She looked down again, not sure how to feel about his comment. "You surprise me, Mr. Darcy—William. See, perhaps that is my problem; I still think of you as Mr. Darcy. But tell me, when did you start thinking of me as Elizabeth?"

He was definitely smiling now. "Oh, I do not recall exactly, but it was sometime between when you defended my sister with your rather impressive rock throwing skills and when you told me off for not noticing that the maid was ill. Yes, definitely during that time."

"You laugh, sir, but I have not forgotten my mortification on either occasion. Well," she continued, considering, "perhaps less mortification for throwing the rocks. Mr. Wickham deserved more than he got in that situation, and I cannot bring myself to truly regret my behavior." They had reached the door to her room and both stopped by mutual decision.

"I should have told you to bring rocks when we went to find Wickham and your sister," Mr. Darcy said. The smile drained off his face to be replaced by a scowl. "They would have served you better than I did." He turned on one heel as if to leave. Even through his coat she could see that he had tensed, hands curled into fists at his sides.

"Mr. Darc—William?" she asked, raising her voice to stop him.

"Yes?" he asked without turning back.   .

"Why did you—well, Georgiana told me you never ride in a carriage with an unmarried lady if you can help it, even when she is present. Why take the chance of bringing me with you, for a girl that you were not connected to and certainly did not like?"

He turned back and met her eyes, gaze intense. "Wickham was my problem to deal with. Your sister would not have been in such a position if I had dealt with him properly the first time—or even the second, when he came to Netherfield. I do not shirk my duties, Elizabeth."

"And I suppose you knew I did not wish to marry you," she said.

To her surprise, he winced slightly at the comment and looked away.

Struck by a sudden fear, she asked hurriedly, "You do not think it was me who notified the paper, surely?"

For a moment, Mr. Darcy did not move. Then he looked up, face back in its unreadable mask. "No, Elizabeth, I don't. I will see you at dinner. Good day." Bowing slightly, he pivoted and left, and this time she did not try to stop him

CHAPTER TWENTY-ONE

They fell into a pattern over the next few weeks. Mr. Darcy was always gone when Elizabeth awoke and made her way to the breakfast room, out inspecting different parts of the estate or shut up in his study with business if the weather was truly abominable. She would eat her toast and drink her tea, then meet with Mrs. Reynolds to go over the household activities of that day and choose the meal for that evening—or, more often, confirm the housekeeper's choice.

Duties done, Elizabeth occasionally went on a short horseback ride with Mr. Darcy to see the greater estate and practice her riding. More often, she would make her way to the chair by the fire in the sitting room and read a book or write letters until she could no longer stand being in one place. Still refraining from indulging in longer walks—as much due to the frigid weather as to a great amount of self-restraint on her part—Lizzy walked laps in the courtyard or galleries, or ventured into the gardens behind the house on warmer days.

Orion, the old white hunting dog, was her only consistent companion, and would curl up at her feet or trot next to her as the activity demanded with equal happiness. He had remained loyally with her since her tour of Pemberley's stables, and Elizabeth occasionally wondered if the dog could sense the immense loneliness that threatened to consume her in unguarded moments.

She ended each afternoon in the music room, slowly working her way through Georgiana's old music. Her skill level did not come close to matching the sheet music that her new sister had left on the piano, but Elizabeth began to feel that with such continual practice she might become truly proficient for the first time in her life.

Then came the evenings, when she would change for dinner and meet her husband outside her rooms to be escorted down to the smaller dining room. They made pleasant, meaningless conversation, and she was always relieved to escape back to the piano, which she played while Mr. Darcy listened. Eventually—she made it a game to guess when it would be each evening—he would stand and say, "Thank you, Elizabeth. Shall we retire now?"

She always agreed, and he escorted her to her door to prepare for the night with the help of Alice. Once Alice had gone, there would be a soft knock on the door that connected their suites, and he would enter to find her sitting in the rocking chair by her fire, waiting for him just as she had been the first night at Pemberley. He always left afterwards, and she fell asleep knowing she would wake to do it all again the next day.

A month and a half after she had arrived at Pemberley, Elizabeth was returning to her rooms after a particularly cold stroll through the gardens. Halfway down the hallway, she paused, noticing that her door stood ajar. She proceeded with more care than usual, glad that Orion had chosen to stay next to the fire in the sitting room rather than brave the cold and wind. She had missed his company, but the lack of clicking toenails on the hallway floor let her approach almost silently.

Elizabeth heard voices as she neared the door and slowed her steps, stopping just outside the door frame. Within seconds, it became apparent to her that at least two maids were within.

"—not like looking after a real lady," one of them was saying. "She doesn't have any interesting dresses, and it's not like anyone cares that we get to do her laundry. She's nearly as much of a nobody as we are—or at least she *was*."

Elizabeth felt like her blood had turned to ice, and covered her mouth with her hand so she wouldn't make any noise.

"Maybe she wears simple dresses since it's just her and Mr. Darcy here at home," the other girl said, then giggled. "Although I thought that surely they would have guests by now, if only for dinner." Another giggle. "Maybe he doesn't want anyone to see her, and that's why they came here instead of staying in Town for the season."

"No, silly, Mrs. Reynolds told me there was some kind of scandal. She was staying with family—in trade, can you imagine *that*? —and something happened so he *had* to marry her. I'd bet that she set it up, whatever it was, and I think Mrs. Reynolds agreed with me even though she told me not to spread rumors. It's obvious she doesn't like Mrs. Darcy; anyone can see that. I wonder what Mr. Darcy told her."

"The scandal must have been awful if he actually married her, my sister in Town says men can get away with nearly anything and not hurt their reputations. It's not like *she* would have been worth it."

Elizabeth took a deep breath and forced herself away from the wall. Moving as quickly and quietly as she could, she made her way back down the hall, re-winding her scarf around her face as she went. Blindly, she back-tracked down the stairs and out into the gardens—and then, for the first time since she left Longbourn, began to run.

The cold air tore at her lungs and numbed her face almost instantly, but Elizabeth bent her head and pushed on. If only she could get out of the view of the house then maybe—*oh Lord, please*— she could be Lizzy Bennet again for an afternoon, happy and secure in who she was, content with her life and ready to find the wit in any situation. How anyone could manage to find wit in her current situation she didn't know, but she ran on anyway, until her lungs burned and a stitch tore at one side.

When she looked up at last, Elizabeth had no idea where she was. The neatly tended gardens had given way to open countryside, and just ahead was a wooded area with trees that tossed and swayed in the wind. Without thinking, she put her head back down and headed for the woods, thinking only of finding a bit of shelter from the biting wind.

The first line of trees did little to block the gusts, so Elizabeth kept walking. After a while it became a mindless process of simply putting one foot in front of another as she wound through the trees. Only when her feet began to go numb did Elizabeth stop and look around with quickly growing horror. Identical trees stared back at her from every direction, and the dead, matted grass beneath her feet showed no discernable tracks. Through the branches above her head, the sky was the same nondescript grey in every direction. Even if she knew what direction lead back to the house, the clouds blocked any sunlight that might have told her which way to turn.

If you are ever caught outdoors in the cold, keep moving, a voice that sounded like her father whispered in her mind. *If you stop, your body cools down and it will be much harder to stay warm.*

Elizabeth took a deep breath to calm herself. She readjusted her pelisse and scarf to make sure they covered as much of her as possible, then picked a direction at random and started walking again.

It seemed like an hour, though she had no way of knowing, before the terrain began to change. The trees continued, but the ground began to slope upwards, and every so often large stones rested between tree trunks. Had she passed stones on her way into the forest? Elizabeth couldn't be sure, but her heart sank at the probability that her new home lay farther away than ever. Would they have missed her by now? Her stomach growled, and she wondered if it was dinner time or if the additional exercise had caused the hunger sooner than usual.

Even if they did miss me, how would anyone know to look here?

Forcing the thoughts out of her mind, Elizabeth continued on. This time, rather than focusing on nothing at all, she began to pray.

The sky had darkened noticeably when she crested a small ridge and found a tiny cabin before her. Sucking in a ragged breath, Lizzy quickened her steps to reach it, then halted. She narrowed her eyes, searching the surrounding landscape for signs of life. Only when she had circled the cabin and found nothing did she approach the door. Surely nothing inside could be worse than freezing to death—could it?

But despite her fears the cabin was empty, and obviously so. There was only one room, containing a rough table and two chairs. *Perhaps it is a hunting cabin?* she wondered as she barred the door from the inside and hurried towards the stone hearth, next to which wood had been piled.

Elizabeth's next half hour was filled with attempts to start a fire using the flint which had been left on top of the wood. Finally, just as she was about to give up, a spark caught and didn't immediately die. Adding wood chips with great care, Lizzy breathed a sigh of relief as her tiny fire grew and she was able to warm her hands. She added slightly larger pieces to the flame and balanced full sized chunks around those, then sat back, wrapped her arms around her knees, and gave in to the tears that had threatened since she overheard the maids.

She cried for all the times she had felt inadequate since coming to Pemberley and for the fear that Mr. Darcy must be just as unhappy with their marriage as she. Mainly, though, Lizzy cried for the girl who had once sworn she would marry only for love and truly believed that such an ending was possible. Well, it wasn't possible now, and she shuddered as she prepared to say goodbye to that girl and her hopes forever.

Eventually, Elizabeth uncurled herself and reached out to tend to the fire again, feeling better for her cry. "Jane always did say I could cry myself silly before my monthlies," she said aloud, trying for a bit of her old humor. Then she froze, counting back the weeks. It was the end of her sixth week at Pemberley, of that she was sure. But before that—had it been one week or two since her monthly bleeding?

"Four weeks," she whispered, all thoughts of humor gone. "It's four weeks late."

Mrs. Gardiner had mentioned this as well, in her last set of instructions and explanations. "Should your husband lie with you and get you with child, your monthlies will stop. You'll likely feel ill as well. Some women feel sick only in the mornings, while others feel it all day. This will pass as the child grows. You might not even notice at first, but I would caution you against saying anything for the first month. The baby will quicken around the fourth month, and then you can be absolutely sure."

Elizabeth took what seemed like her hundredth deep breath of the day. "Okay," she murmured to herself. "Fourth month versus fourth week. I don't feel sick at all. Calm down, Lizzy. Keep yourself alive now, you can worry about a baby later—once you get home."

The fire had warmed the air in the cabin slightly, and Elizabeth removed the scarf from around her neck, folding it so it could be used as a pillow. The single window in the cabin showed that night had fallen, turning the sky outside black. The combined exercise and exposure to the cold had exhausted Elizabeth, and she sleepily piled more of the wood onto the fire, then pulled her pelisse more tightly around herself and laid down with her head on the scarf. Within moments, she was asleep.

A loud banging on the door awakened her some time later, and she sat up with a start, eyes searching the room for something that she could use as a weapon if the person had less than honest intentions. She snatched up the old, rusted poker from next to the fire and turned to look at the door with wide eyes.

Did someone from Pemberley manage to find me? It seemed unlikely—how could they have done so in the dark, with no indication of where she had gone? Perhaps the usual occupant of the cabin had returned. Perhaps, perhaps—

The person outside banged on the door again, and Elizabeth rolled into a crouching position, turning her eyes to the single small window in the cabin wall. Whoever it was would have been able to see the light from her fire, but the table stood between the window and where she had lay. The thought calmed her slightly. She shuddered at the idea of someone watching her while she slept.

"Whoever you are, open the door!" a man yelled from outside, and Elizabeth tensed. "There is a missing person on the estate and I will not leave until I have searched this cabin!"

Lizzy stood, staring at the backside of the door as if it could reveal who stood on the other side. To speak would be to reveal herself as a woman, but the tone and language were that of a gentleman. In fact, it sounded very much like Mr. Darcy, though she had never heard him yell before.

"Who is there?" she called back, doing her best to lower the pitch of her voice.

There was a pregnant pause. "Elizabeth?" the man said, and this time she was sure that the man outside was her husband.

"Yes," she responded, hurrying over to remove the piece of wood holding the door closed.

He pushed the door open before she had stepped away, and she stumbled backwards, catching herself on the table. Darcy blew into the room with Orion on his heels and slammed the door closed against the wind, re-barring it behind them.

"Elizabeth," he said again, taking a single stride towards her and pulling her into a tight hold. "Oh God, Elizabeth," he said into her hair, moving slightly so he could pull her even closer. For a moment they simply stood there, and she could feel his heart beating fast and hard against her ear. Then suddenly, for the second time that night, Elizabeth began to cry.

CHAPTER TWENTY-TWO

Mr. Darcy drew back immediately, moving one of his hands from Elizabeth's back to her cheek and gently wiping away her tears with a thumb. She moved her head back and away, looking fixedly at the ground so he couldn't see her face.

Very gently, Mr. Darcy walked both of them around the table so they stood before the fire. "Sit," he said softly, and she lowered herself to the floor and pulled her legs up to her chest, sure she was about to receive a reprimand for running off.

To her immense surprise, he lowered himself to the ground as well and settled behind her with his back against the table. Spreading his legs out to either side, Darcy pulled her back so that she rested against his chest and wrapped his arms around her again. "All right," he murmured. "Tell me what happened to send you out here on one of the coldest days of the year."

She tucked her head down, knowing it was cowardice but not yet willing to face him and admit the extent of her inadequacy.

"Did you get bad news from Longbourn?"

She shook her head once.

"Are you homesick?"

She paused, but missing home had not driven her out here, so she gave another shake of her head.

"Did I do something to hurt you?"

She raised her head slightly. "No. It wasn't you."

"Who was it?" he asked, smoothing the hair back from her face. "Elizabeth, who hurt you?" At her silence, he persisted. "It was someone at Pemberley, then?"

Not willing to lie, even though she hated the idea of telling him, Elizabeth unfolded herself slightly. "There were two maids. They—well, it's nothing I haven't thought myself, but they said I wasn't good enough to be your wife, and that—" she stopped abruptly.

"That what?" he asked.

"That you brought me to Pemberley because you were ashamed of me, and that's why we haven't returned to Town or invited anyone even for dinner," she whispered, feeling more tears slide down her cheeks.

"Was that all they said?" Mr. Darcy asked, a rumble in his voice that hadn't been there before.

"One of them said that I caused a scandal on purpose so you would have to marry me. Mrs. Reynolds thinks so too."

"She would never!" Darcy burst out.

"No, she does," Lizzy said, sitting up slightly more and swiping mindlessly at her tears. "She hates me. The only time she is even remotely pleasant to me is when you are there."

Darcy took a deep breath. "Why didn't you tell me before?"

She looked away, watching the flames. "Because I knew you didn't wish to marry me, and I didn't want to cause you any more problems. I thought that you would not want to be bothered."

"Why did you think that?" he asked, voice emotionless.

"Well, because I knew—"

"No," he said, cutting her off. "Why did you think I didn't want to marry you?"

Now she was truly caught off guard. "Because ever since I met you I have been nothing but impertinent and unladylike. Because you seemed so uncomfortable and reticent whenever we met. Because it was obvious to me that you only looked at me to find fault."

He took a deep, shuddering breath and leaned back. "My God, Elizabeth, is that what you've thought this whole time?"

"Yes," she said, hearing the confusion in her voice. What else had he expected her to think, when his opinion had seemed so marked?

Darcy laughed, but there was little humor in the sound. In fact, it sounded downright strangled. "Elizabeth," he said, and she felt him bring a hand up behind her to rub his face. "I've been in love with you since we arrived in London." She swiveled around to stare at him, incredulous, and he added, "At least."

"You—you were in love with me," she said slowly, "when I imposed on your hospitality, insulted you to your face in front of your sister and servant, involved you in my sister's highly undesirable situation, and managed to create a scandal that required matrimony to solve. You told my uncle it had been a mistake to take me with you when we found Lydia, and that you wouldn't even *talk* to me for fear of furthering that error. And then in the whole month and a half that we've been married, you haven't said a single thing to me besides what was necessary!"

Darcy sighed. "I know. I can explain myself, if you'll let me do so. I'm not even going to ask how you heard that."

She raised an eyebrow, feeling a sliver of her old spirit returning to her. "Go ahead."

237

He looked away and took several moments before speaking. "I did not want to like you. I tried to avoid you in Hertfordshire, especially when we were together at Netherfield. Doubtless that is why you first decided I did not like you, for I did my best to discourage any interaction between us."

"Why?" she asked, frowning. "Sorry, go on."

He sighed again. "Because I thought you beneath me. Your father's situation, your mother's connections to trade, your sisters' behavior—all of this I held against any possible chance of a marriage between us. And yet I could not get you out of my mind. Every time we met you fascinated me. I have been surrounded for years by women who will change everything about themselves for the chance to gain my favor, and you seemed to delight in disagreeing with me."

"So why did you stop trying to forget me? Or did you?" she could not help but ask.

"You will laugh, but it was Lady Catherine's outburst that made up my mind. Hearing all of the awful things she shouted at you, things *I* had thought, made me realize how little any of them mattered. I walked into that room ready to declare myself, and only remembered at the last moment that I had not spoken to you yet." He paused. "I would have come to see your uncle the next day even if that article hadn't been in the paper, to ask his permission to court you properly."

"Perhaps someday I will laugh," Elizabeth said, "but I must confess myself rather overwhelmed at the moment." A tear trickled down her cheek.

"Elizabeth, sweet, don't cry," Darcy said immediately, reaching up to wipe it away.

"I don't know why I'm crying! Oh, it all makes so much more sense now! Your reaction when Mr. Wickham—"

"I wanted to kill him more in that moment than I ever had before. To see him with his hands on you, when I still had to be a gentleman—" he broke off, shaking his head. "I hope to never again feel what I did then."

"What did you mean by what you told my uncle?" she asked, suddenly remembering the words that had stopped her cold. "That you would not talk to me? I didn't mean to eavesdrop, but I was passing by and heard my name. You seemed so adamant."

"I may as well tell you all of it, although I had not wanted to. I met with your uncle to convince him to allow me to pay Wickham's debts, and secure him a new commission far away from London or Hertfordshire."

"No!" she exclaimed, twisting around again to look at him better.

"Yes. Had I dealt with him to begin with, when he hurt Georgiana, he never could have fooled you or any of your sisters—or any other young lady. At least, that is what I told myself. The truth is I would have done anything to keep you from looking like you did when the news came about Lydia. I did not want you to know, because I did not want it to color any feelings you had for me. If you came to care for me, I did not want it to be from a sense of obligation."

Elizabeth shook her head and leaned into him slightly, tears coming faster now. "I never knew, any of it. I had no idea. Oh, why can't I quit crying? I never—" She froze, her realization about the possibility of a child coming back to her. Would pregnancy alter her emotions? Had her aunt said anything about that? She couldn't remember.

"Dearest?" Mr. Darcy asked, pulling her closer and looking down to see her face better at the same time. "What is it?"

She took a deep breath. "Very well. You have been honest with me, so I suppose I cannot keep a secret from you in good faith. I—well, you must understand that I don't know, for sure. But I, we—I may be with child. I won't know really for a while, but—"

Elizabeth stopped, feeling her face flame with heat. A second later Darcy's arms tightened around her even more, lifting her up to sit on his lap.

"That," he said, "is the second best thing I've heard today."

She turned into him a bit more and leaned her head against his shoulder tentatively. "What was the first?"

"Hearing your voice through that door," he said. "I was so worried about you. I didn't even ask, are you well? Are you hurt at all, or still cold? Will the baby be harmed?"

"I'm fine," she said, closing her eyes and relishing in how safe and warm it was in his arms. "And if there is a baby, it should be fine as long as I am—and provided I get food in the next day or two. How did you even find me?"

"Orion," Mr. Darcy said, turning to look at the old dog. Orion had laid himself down to one side of the fire, and seeing that their attention had turned to him, gave two thumps of his tail. "I came back from my ride and he was laying in front of the fire in my study. I haven't seen him away from you more than twice since we arrived at Pemberley, so I went looking for you. When I couldn't find you inside, a footman told me you had been walking in the gardens earlier. We went out to look and Orion caught your scent immediately. I didn't even think to bring food."

"I was so worried no one would know where to look, and I don't think I could find my way back,"

Elizabeth said. "I took off without paying any attention to where I was going." She gave a short laugh. "The last time I did that was after Mr. Collins' proposal, but at least then I had prior knowledge of the landscape! It was a strike of luck finding this cabin." Feeling exhausted again now that the adrenaline had drained out of her system, Elizabeth yawned.

"Orion will lead us home tomorrow," Mr. Darcy said. "For now, you should sleep if you can."

She nodded against his chest. "So should you. I'm so glad you found me, William."

"That's the first time you've called me William that it hasn't sounded forced," he said.

"It's hard to think of you as the proud, odious Mr. Darcy when you seem so set on being agreeable," she told him with a smile. "'William' is much more fitting for this conversation. Whenever I thought of you as Mr. Darcy I could almost hear Caroline Bingley praising everything you did. 'Why Mr. Darcy, you write uncommonly fast!'" she said in a high voice, smiling at him. "'Oh Mr. Darcy, you are so rich and dignified! Please notice me, Mr. Darcy!'"

Darcy burst out laughing. "Elizabeth, I don't know how I ever thought I was happy before you," he said. "Here," he reached into a coat pocket and pulled out a letter. "You just reminded me—I have news that you will like."

He handed over the letter and she seized it curiously, unfolding the paper to find an unruly scrawl.

Darcy –

I am delighted to inform you that Miss Jane Bennet has made me the happiest of men by accepting my hand in marriage. She is truly an angel! We are to marry in roughly a month's time, but are in complete agreeance that no wedding would be complete without you and the lovely Mrs. Darcy. Please advise if you will be available to come to Hertfordshire in early April. My most sincere congratulations again on your marriage—and we are now to be brothers! But I digress. I daresay Jane will provide more of the particulars when she writes to your wife. I confess that I see any time away from my angel a waste, and so will end here.

Your friend,

Charles Bingley

P.S. Will you stand up with me?

Elizabeth laughed as she read, then looked up at her husband. "Oh, William, I am so happy for them! We will go, won't we? I should hate to miss Jane's wedding."

"Of course we shall go, unless the doctor says it is unsafe for you to travel."

She quirked an eyebrow at him. "I believe you will have me wrapped up in blankets and treat me as though I am glass until this child arrives—if there even is one!"

They had shifted away somewhat, and he tucked her back in close to him. "That is a wonderful idea. Blankets it shall be, and meals will be brought up on a tray so you need not exert yourself, and—"

He broke off and looked down at her, eyes laughing. "And of course I jest, for I shudder to think what you would do locked up in a single room for longer than a day, Elizabeth."

Elizabeth laughed, then frowned as she remembered another question that had been on her mind for some time. "William?"

"Yes?"

"What did my father say to you the day we left for London? You both looked so serious, and since Papa so seldom is I have wondered ever since."

"Ah," he tipped his head back and smiled a bit. "He said, and I quote, 'Do make sure you take care of my daughter. I am rather fond of her, and should not like to find she ran from one man not worthy of her to another.' I have had several occasions to think on that comment and wonder if he thinks that I have kept the promise I made to do so."

Elizabeth yawned again. "I am sure he will have something to say to both of us at Jane's wedding, but he cannot deny that I am happy with you as I never would have been with Mr. Collins."

Darcy pulled his greatcoat off and adjusted his scarf with Elizabeth's so that they formed a single long pillow, then laid down and opened his arms to her. "Good," he said as she slid into them. "I would not have you unhappy for anything, Elizabeth."

She snuggled in closer, tendrils of sleep already reaching out to cloud her thoughts. "William?" she asked again.

"Yes, dearest?"

"Will you call me Lizzy? I feel like I'm in trouble when you call me Elizabeth all the time."

"I would love to." He pulled his greatcoat over them like a blanket and kissed her forehead. "Sleep well, Lizzy."

CHAPTER TWENTY-THREE

The sun was shining when Elizabeth awoke the next morning. The fire had died down overnight and the cabin was chilly, but tucked up next to Mr. Darcy she was perfectly warm. Gleeful to find him still asleep, she turned to study her husband's face unguarded for the first time.

Unfortunately for her studies, his eyes opened moments later. He blinked once, then a smile spread across his entire face. "I have wished to wake up like this for so long," he whispered.

"And I have wished that you would stay with me," she responded, reaching up to touch his face with her fingertips. "William, why didn't you ever tell me how you felt?"

"I meant to," Darcy said. "You seemed different, quiet and uncertain, during our journey to Pemberley and so I decided I would wait until you had relaxed and begun to feel more at home. I meant to do so after we toured the stables. And then you made the comment that I had known you did not want to marry me." He looked away, then back. "I thought that I would give you time to feel more like I did, and I tried to give you space."

"I thought you were avoiding me," she said with a giggle, beginning to see the humor in the situation.

"Never," he said, standing up and reaching down to help her to her feet, which turned into pulling her into a tight embrace. He bent down to kiss her, not breaking the kiss until they were both breathless. "Never, Lizzy."

They put out what remained of the fire and bundled themselves up against the cold, then left the cabin to make the long trek back to Pemberley.

"Go home, Orion," Mr. Darcy told the dog once they had closed the door behind them. "Home."

Orion gave a sharp bark and trotted forward, tail lifted and ears perked like a much younger dog. He went several yards before looking back over his shoulder and giving another short bark.

Elizabeth laughed. "Yes, we're coming, Orion."

The return journey was far more enjoyable than the previous day's solitary walk had been. Darcy and Elizabeth talked the entire way, discussing lighter topics to begin with and gradually growing more serious as Pemberley came into view. Elizabeth was slightly apprehensive about facing the staff that thought so low of her. Darcy was livid.

"I had not thought to ask—will they be looking for you as well?" she asked as they reached the edge of the gardens and could see a flurry of activity surrounding the house.

Mr. Darcy laughed. "You know, they probably will be. I had not even considered it. My only concern was you." He lifted an arm and waived at one of the people in back of the house. The man gave a shout, calling something back to his companion and then jogging towards them.

Lizzy hesitated without meaning to, and Darcy reached out to her immediately, wrapping one of his arms around her waist and pulling her close. "It will be okay," he murmured, kissing the top of her head. "You don't have to feel alone anymore, and we'll work through this. Now, head up. Where's the young lady who confronted Mr. Wickham with rocks and put me in my place for mistreating a maid?"

She took a deep breath and smiled up at him. "She's on her best behavior, sir."

"Well, tell her to quit it," Darcy said. "I miss my impertinent minx."

Elizabeth laughed and let herself be propelled forward again, still tucked into Darcy's side.

"Mr. Darcy!" The footman skidded to a stop in front of them. "Are you okay, sir?" He glanced at Elizabeth, then back to Mr. Darcy, seemingly still unsure what to make of her. "And Mrs. Darcy?" he added.

"We are both fine, thank you," Mr. Darcy said. "Is there a search party out looking for us?"

"Yes, sir, they left just after dawn. We did not realize you were gone until after dark last night, and did not want to start looking with no clues." He looked slightly sheepish as he finished his sentence.

"Understandable. Last night was brutally cold, and I am glad my men were not out in it. Please send out several men after the searchers, preferably in pairs and on horseback. I do not want any more people missing tonight."

"Very wise, sir," the footman said, giving a half bow. Turning, he ran back towards the house to execute the order.

Mrs. Reynolds was the next person to arrive, with three maids and the butler just behind her. "Oh, Mr. Darcy! We were so worried! You should have told someone where you went, or taken someone with you. I am glad your mother did not have to live through the suspense of trying to find you!"

"I could hardly leave my wife out in the cold, and she did not have a prior knowledge of the land or a companion with a fine nose as I did," Darcy said, voice noticeably cooler than when he had spoken to the footman. "Would you have had me leave her in the elements so that I might sleep warm in my bed?" He walked forwards with Elizabeth held snug against him, and the welcoming party made room for them to pass.

"Why, of course not," Mrs. Reynolds exclaimed, hurrying to catch up and then walking alongside the couple. "But I will take her to task as well! What were you thinking, Mrs. Darcy, to disappear in such a manner? You may have done that before, but surely you understand that there are different standards for you now!"

Mr. Darcy stopped mid-stride, catching Lizzy so that she stopped with him. The rest of the party was left to stumble to a halt on their own.

"Mrs. Reynolds, you will desist immediately. We will see you in our private sitting room once we have changed into fresh clothes and had something to eat. Until that time, you are better off seeing that warm water and food are sent to our rooms than you are spouting opinions that were not asked for."

Mrs. Reynolds opened her mouth to retort, but Mr. Darcy cut her off with one of his most haughty and disdainful looks. She snapped her mouth closed again, two spots of color flaring on her cheeks.

"She will see me as the person who ruined the agreeable relationship you had with each other," Elizabeth said softly, once Darcy's long strides had propelled them ahead of the others.

"You are my wife, my love, and the future mother of my children," he replied, the trace of anger that was still in his voice fading as he looked

251

down at her. "There is not even a choice to make between the two of you. Mrs. Reynolds has long held my respect and affection by managing Pemberley competently while never resorting to the mean tactics I have seen other upper servants occasionally employ. Not once have I questioned that she truly cares. If she cannot extend that same care to you, then we will find someone who can."

"She was worried for you," Lizzy said, her honest nature asserting itself.

"Yes, and in retrospect I can understand some of her worry. What I cannot understand nor forgive is that she let unconfirmed personal vendettas directly interfere with her duties of housekeeper. Do not fight me on this, Elizabeth. I will not have you made to feel unworthy in your own home."

They had reached the house, and entered to a bevy of greetings and exclamations of relief. Darcy responded succinctly, reassuring all present and giving instructions while continually moving Elizabeth down the hall and up the stairs to their quarters. At last, only Elizabeth's maid Alice stood several feet away, waiting to attend to her mistress.

Darcy stopped in front of Elizabeth's door and looked down at her, obviously reluctant to release his hold on her.

She smiled up at him. "Go. Alice will take good care of me, and I'll see you in our sitting room once I am refreshed."

He relaxed slightly and she realized that they had never discussed Alice—no doubt he had wondered if she was another of the servants who had treated Elizabeth poorly. He gave a nod and dropped a kiss on her forehead before stepping away. "I will see you soon."

Alice was efficient, and in less than half an hour Elizabeth opened the door to the sitting room that connected her room to her husband's feeling remarkably better. This private sitting room was all but unknown to her. Darcy had pointed it out during her initial brief tour of the house, but she had not entered it since. The door leading into it had simply become, in her mind, the portal through which Mr. Darcy emerged each night.

Looking at the room now, Elizabeth found a pleasant, simply adorned chamber. A small table stood in the middle of the room, upon which a tray of cold meats, cheese, and fruit rested. There were two comfortable-looking chairs in front of the small fireplace, and a small bookcase held a collection of much-loved books. Elizabeth's curiosity was immediately piqued, and she resolved to make a study of the books her husband saw fit to keep separate from Pemberley's official library at a later time.

For now, she joined Mr. Darcy at the table. They did not speak beyond a brief greeting until between them they had consumed nearly all of the food provided.

Finally, Darcy looked up and smiled. "I do not believe I have ever seen you eat that much. Do you feel better now?"

She blushed slightly, self-conscious, but smiled back. "Much better."

"Good. If you ever go missing again, God forbid, I will think to bring food with me."

A knock sounded on the door, and Mr. Darcy raised an eyebrow at Elizabeth, asking silently if she was ready to deal with Mrs. Reynolds. She nodded, and he called, "Enter."

A maid came in first, followed closely by the housekeeper. Mrs. Reynolds stopped just inside the door and folded her hands in front of her, awaiting further instructions. Only after the maid had collected the plates and remaining food and exited the room again did Mr. Darcy speak.

"Sit," he said, gesturing to one of the unoccupied chairs at the table. Slowly, Mrs. Reynolds did as he had directed.

For several long seconds, silence reigned. Mrs. Reynolds looked distinctly uncomfortable.

Elizabeth schooled her features into a blank mask similar to the one she had seen Darcy wear so often.

He made no such effort to conceal his displeasure. "Mrs. Reynolds, I would explain the cause of my displeasure, but you are an intelligent woman. No doubt you already have a good guess as to why you are here."

The housekeeper frowned. "I would hear it from you to ensure that we understand each other."

The corner of Darcy's mouth twitched, but it was not the happy movement that Elizabeth had seen before. This time, he looked distinctly dangerous, and Lizzy's estimation of Mrs. Reynolds' backbone grew when the woman didn't appear phased.

"I am speaking of your atrocious treatment of *my wife* over the past month and a half that we have been in residence. Of all the people at Pemberley, I thought I could count on you. You have let me down to the extreme. Not only did you leave Elizabeth to fend for herself as often as you could arrange, you snubbed her and allowed others to speak poorly of her in your presence. I do not know why you thought such behavior was acceptable, but you were wrong."

Mrs. Reynolds opened her mouth angrily, then closed it again.

"You thought me unworthy of him and as such not entitled to your respect," Elizabeth said quietly, folding her hands on her lap. "You thought I trapped Mr. Darcy into a marriage he did not want, and you thought to punish me for it."

Again, Mrs. Reynolds' mouth opened and closed.

"Do you mean to gasp for air like a fish, or are you going to answer Mrs. Darcy?" Mr. Darcy asked, voice cool.

The housekeeper looked down, and her knuckles turned white as she gripped the seat of her chair. When she spoke, it started softly. "I've spent your whole life helping raise you to be a good master and a good man. I've wondered many a time what kind of a wife you would bring home, and I have prayed she would be good enough for you."

Her voice rose. "But you brought a nobody, and not only did you hardly speak to her, but there were whispers of a scandal, too many to simply be ignored! Of course I was disappointed for you, and less than willing to help your *wife*!" She spat out the final word. "She was the one who wanted this enough to trap you, I figured she could learn the ropes on her own."

"I caused the scandal, Mrs. Reynolds," Darcy said quietly. "Not Elizabeth."

Elizabeth opened her mouth and turned sharply to her husband, ready to remind him that Lydia had truly been the cause, not him. He looked back at her patiently, and she read *I asked you to go to that inn* in his gaze.

She gave him her own look back—*I wouldn't have let you stop me*—but said nothing aloud.

Darcy kept his eyes on Lizzy, but his words were to Mrs. Reynolds. "You have Elizabeth to thank for the fact that I am not dismissing you right now."

He turned to the housekeeper. "You had no right to judge my wife with only gossip for information. You certainly had no right to treat her poorly, no matter what your personal feelings on my marriage. You have been my most trusted servant, but if you treat her with anything other than the utmost respect and deference from here on out, I will ask you to leave Pemberley. Any choice that involves Elizabeth is not a choice."

There was a tap on the door, and after a pause in which Mr. Darcy fixed Mrs. Reynolds with an unwaveringly stern gaze, he called, "Come in."

The door opened and the same footman who had met them in the garden stepped in. "The doctor that you requested has arrived from Lambton, sir."

"Thank you," Mr. Darcy said. "Please show him up."

The footman bowed and exited. When he had gone, Darcy turned back to Mrs. Reynolds. "Do you understand me?" he asked.

She looked like she was sucking on a lemon, but Mrs. Reynolds nodded. "Yes, sir."

"If you have concerns in the future, come to me and we will discuss anything within reason. For now, consider yourself dismissed."

Mrs. Reynolds nodded again and stood, then hesitated. "Is anything amiss, Mr. Darcy?" she asked. "I have not known you to call a doctor in the past."

Darcy's face gave nothing away. "As I believe you made clear earlier, I have done numerous things in the past month that you have not known me to do in the past. The doctor is a precaution. If you would be so kind as to leave us?"

"I do not remember you requesting a doctor," Elizabeth remarked once Mrs. Reynolds had gone.

"I believe it was in the midst of about eight other people asking after our health, so I can't blame you."

"William, I don't even know if there is a child. It is nothing more than a guess at the moment."

"All the more reason to consult a doctor," he replied, then smiled at her stubborn impression. "Humor me, my love. I have been dreadfully worried about you." He stood and walked over to stand behind her, dropping a kiss on her forehead and rubbing her shoulders lightly. "I promise it won't be worse than spending a night out of doors in a Derbyshire winter. And I will stay with you the whole time if you would like."

She smiled up at him just as voices sounded outside the door. "I would like."

CHAPTER TWENTY-FOUR

That night, when Darcy entered her chamber, Elizabeth stood and met him halfway between the door and her chair at the fireplace. He caught her up in his arms and held her tightly against him for some time before leaning down to kiss her.

"I used to dream about you greeting me like this," he admitted in a whisper, resting his forehead against hers.

"Oh, William," she laughed quietly. "Apparently all we needed was a cold night in a nearly empty cabin. Who would have guessed that all this—" she gestured at the room around them— "would be such a detriment to our happiness."

Darcy kissed her again. "You, my dear, are an impertinent minx." Continuing to kiss her, he walked her slowly backwards towards the bed.

She pulled back when her legs hit the mattress. "I take it this means you were satisfied with what the doctor had to say?" Darcy had explained the situation to the doctor that afternoon and stayed with her while the man performed his examination. Then the men had retired for a conversation, and Elizabeth had suspected at the time that marital relations would be one of the topics they discussed.

"Quite satisfied," he said, turning his attention to kissing her neck.

"Anything else I should be aware of?" she asked when she could breathe again.

"Hmmm," he said, moving his kisses down to her shoulders and sliding her dressing robe off for better access. "I believe there was something about making sure you had plenty of rest, obviously with myself for company," he glanced up and she caught the corner of his grin. "And yes, I am to dote on you and attend to your comfort at all times. I am quite your servant, madam."

She drew back further, which meant sitting down on the bed, and reached a hand up to his face. "That is quite disappointing, sir, for I was hoping to find a husband rather than a servant."

He grinned. "I believe a husband can be arranged, madam." Shedding his shirt, he followed her down onto the bed and continued kissing her.

"William?" she said, breathless.

"Yes, my Lizzy?"

"I didn't know it could be like this. That I could feel like this."

He kissed her lips. "Shall we see how much better it can get?"

She nodded with anticipation, and for Mr. and Mrs. Darcy, the rest of the world ceased to exist.

Later, when they were both spent, Elizabeth rolled onto her side and propped herself up on one elbow. Normally, Mr. Darcy would have left by now, but nothing seemed normal tonight.

"Elizabeth," he whispered, looking up at her face. "My Elizabeth."

She smiled, then bit her lip, feeling shy. "Will you stay, William?"

He pulled her close against him, tucking her into his arms so her head was pillowed on his shoulder. "Do you want me to?"

"I've wanted you to from the first night."

"What fools we have been," he said. "Well, I have been the fool. I cannot blame you for your uncertainty, and I won't have anyone speak ill of you, even if it is myself."

She snorted. "I would argue, but it seems to be against my best interest to do so. Very well then, sir, neglect my follies. My good qualities are under your protection, and you are to exaggerate them as much as possible; and, in return, it belongs to me to find occasions for teasing and quarrelling with you as often as may be."

He laughed. "How I have missed your lively teasing and quarrelling, Lizzy. I am most pleased with the arrangement you suggest."

She giggled and tucked herself in more closely, and they talked quietly in the dark about nothing and everything until both of them fell asleep.

*

Elizabeth enjoyed her husband's company in the breakfast room for the first time the next morning, and found the place to be far more pleasant with his company. They had just finished their breakfast when Mrs. Reynolds found them.

"A carriage and rider have been sighted entering the park," she said with a curtsey. "Shall I change the menu for this evening due to our guests?"

To Elizabeth's surprise, the question was directed at her, and she hesitated more from shock than lack of an answer. "I suppose that will depend on who it is," she managed after a moment's pause.

"I must have forgotten to tell you in the commotion of the last few days," Mr. Darcy said. "I believe the carriage will bring Georgiana, although I am unsure of the rider's identity. It is not unheard of for Colonel Fitzwilliam to accompany her, although I had not heard of such a plan from him."

"I hope it is Colonel Fitzwilliam," Elizabeth said. "It would be wonderful to see both he and Georgiana again."

Darcy laughed. "With you here, they'll scarcely notice me. Colonel Fitzwilliam seemed quite enamored with you at our wedding, and Georgiana goes without saying. Actually, I believe I'll be in my study. If you'll call me for dinner?"

He took two steps before Elizabeth caught his arm and pulled him to a stop. "You wouldn't dare," she told her husband, laughing as well.

He grinned down at her. "You're right. I'm not sure I like the idea of you being away from me when there are other men around—even if it is just my cousin."

Elizabeth quirked an eyebrow. "Assuming it is the Colonel. What if the rider is someone else? You had better come with me to greet them."

Darcy gave her a half bow in acquiescence, and as they turned towards the door, Lizzy caught sight of Mrs. Reynolds' face. The older woman seemed astounded at the exchange she had just witnessed, although she collected herself quickly. "You are acquainted with Miss Georgiana, ma'am?" she asked as she followed Darcy and Elizabeth from the room.

"Oh, yes," Elizabeth said. "I met her when she was in Hertfordshire, and we traveled to London together."

"Where Georgiana actually expressed interest in spending time with Elizabeth rather than simply playing her pianoforte," Darcy added as they walked down the stairs. He turned back to Lizzy. "I look forward to seeing her flourish under your guidance."

Elizabeth gave a short laugh. "Let us hope that she does not follow my example in all ways," she said. "I can think of several of my mannerisms that I would not wish on any young lady."

They had reached the front doors, and stepped outside to wait for their guests to arrive. Darcy tucked his arm around Elizabeth and pulled her close against him to shield her from the cold air. "I wouldn't change a thing about you," he said. "My sister would do well to absorb come of your spirit."

On the other side of the steps, Mrs. Reynolds looked flabbergasted.

Luckily, the new arrivals reached the house soon, and before long everyone was back in the warmth of the front hall. The rider *had* been Colonel Fitzwilliam, accompanying Georgiana in one of the Darcy carriages. Mrs. Reynolds bustled off to ready their rooms, and Georgiana soon followed her to freshen up after her long journey.

As soon as Georgiana had left, Colonel Fitzwilliam turned to Darcy. "I have news that you should hear about a certain *friend* of ours," he said quietly. "Shall we go to your study?"

Darcy nodded and offered his arm to Elizabeth. When the Colonel looked surprised, Darcy said, "If you speak of Wickham, as I assume you do, Elizabeth is well aware of his character. I doubt you will say anything that could surprise her."

Colonel Fitzwilliam's face said he thought otherwise, but he remained silent until they reached the study and all had been seated.

"I will not keep you in suspense," he began, "but be advised that I bring bad news."

"Lydia," Elizabeth whispered, thoughts immediately going to her sister.

"What has he done now?" Mr. Darcy demanded.

The Colonel looked between the two of them. "He is dead," he said simply.

Elizabeth sat back in shock. Darcy, on the other hand, immediately leaned forward. "How?" he demanded.

"It was a duel over a game of cards," Colonel Fitzwilliam told them, sounding tired. "As I understand it, Wickham was drunk and losing. He accused his opponent of cheating, perhaps from desperation. The man challenged him to a duel. Wickham was shot in the middle of the chest. He died quickly."

"Lydia?" Elizabeth asked.

"I saw her safely returned to your aunt and uncle," Colonel Fitzwilliam said. "She was," he hesitated, and Elizabeth braced herself for bad news. "She seemed in less than ideal health and spirit, but should recover well with proper care and attention. I have a letter for you from your aunt." He fished the letter out of his coat pocket and handed it over.

"She was hurt?" Lizzy asked, seizing the letter and holding it tightly.

The Colonel looked at Mr. Darcy and something passed between them silently.

"Wickham lacks—*lacked*—the ability to take care of those around him as he ought," Darcy said. "No doubt Lydia has been living a rougher life than she expected upon marrying him. Read your letter. We have details to discuss that do not concern you as immediately, and likely your aunt will have included information that Richard does not know."

Elizabeth hesitated, unsure if he meant for her to leave or not. Seeing her dilemma, Darcy waved a hand towards a chair by the window. "The light there is better for reading. It is where I often attend to my own correspondence."

She gave him a small smile and removed to the chair he indicated, feeling something hot burning in her chest. Most men would have dismissed a wife outright, if they even allowed her into the study in

267

the first place. Darcy had left that choice up to her, and she could not help but realize how lucky she had been by marrying him.

Dear Lizzy,

I will not dissemble, for I am sure you are most alarmed by Colonel Fitzwilliam's news. Lydia is well—or, I should say, will be well. She is better already for a good scrubbing and full night's sleep, and much of the rest will mend soon. I try not to speak ill of the dead, but Mr. Wickham was not a good husband to her. Luckily, she seems more shocked than truly harmed.

What concerns me most is Lydia's report that she has not had her monthlies in nearly three months' time. Am I selfish, Lizzy, to be glad that I can confide in you as I cannot with your mother? I had hoped for her to be truly free of this experience, although I never would have chosen such an end to her marriage, even disliking Mr. Wickham as I did. It does give me comfort to know that any child would have a legitimate name.

Enough of my worries. Time will tell what the future holds, and Lydia has behaved far more maturely in the day she has been with us than I have ever seen in the past. I believe her time away from the shelter of Longbourn taught her about the world, and she may be better off for it, no matter how dark the outlook is now.

I will end here, for Colonel Fitzwilliam is waiting. The man has been an unexpected blessing, and I do hope you will ensure he has good food and rest when he reaches you, for I daresay he has had little of either in the past few days.

Your loving aunt,

Madeline Gardiner

Elizabeth read the letter twice, then turned to observe the Colonel. He did look haggard, she noted. Making up her mind, she stood and went to the door. A passing maid took her request for refreshments and dropped a curtsey, promising to return soon.

Darcy raised an eyebrow when she returned. "My aunt says I am to ensure that Colonel

Fitzwilliam is well fed, and I have yet to see her give an instruction that does not make good sense," Elizabeth said.

The Colonel grinned at his cousin. "I must say I appreciate a woman's touch in your house already, Darce." He turned to Elizabeth. "In all my days at Pemberley, food has never been offered so expediently."

Darcy smiled up at Elizabeth and for a moment she thought he would reach for her. Instead, he nodded towards her original chair and she was both relieved and disappointed as she settled into it. He turned his smile back to Colonel Fitzwilliam, and it took on a joking air. "I must admit I tried to be my usual grumpy self to begin with, but Elizabeth managed to convince me that a woman's touch is just what was needed."

The Colonel gave a single nod, merriment sparkling in his eyes. He mouthed something to Darcy, who grinned. It took Elizabeth a moment longer to understand, but then she smiled as well.

I told you so.

Chapter Twenty-Five

Colonel Fitzwilliam and Darcy had decided that Georgiana should be given a day to rest before they told her the news about Wickham. Elizabeth reluctantly agreed, although Georgiana's anger over the last time they had shielded her from information did not leave her mind. Seeing how exhausted the young lady was after her three days of travel, however, Elizabeth did have to admit that Darcy knew his sister's needs better than herself.

They spent the evening quietly. After dinner, Georgiana and Elizabeth made their way to the informal sitting room while the men rejoined in the library. Typically, Lizzy wouldn't have expected the separation of the sexes with such a small, informal party, but she understood that there were likely more details concerning Wickham that needed to be hashed out.

"Oh Lizzy, I am so glad that you married William!" Georgiana burst out once they were comfortably seated, breaking through Elizabeth's thoughts. "I feel as though I really can call you Lizzy now, without fear of anyone thinking it improper. What do you think of Pemberley? Isn't it wonderful? I think you will love the spring here, when it finally warms up and everything starts to grow again." She stopped abruptly and frowned. "I just remembered, I overheard one of the maids, when she thought I was asleep."

Elizabeth tensed, fearful of what awful rumors Georgiana might repeat.

"She said something about a doctor coming to see you after you were out in the cold—what did she mean?"

Elizabeth relaxed slightly. "I must confess, I wandered off the other day and became quite lost. Luckily I found an old cabin and was able to make a fire for warmth until your brother found me and brought me home."

"Oh no!" Georgiana exclaimed.

"I am quite well, but William was worried," Lizzy said. It was the first time she had said her husband's name to anyone but him, and it felt strange on her tongue.

"William always worries," Georgiana said, nodding. "I have always thought—" she broke off and blushed.

"Yes?" Elizabeth prompted, raising an eyebrow and smiling at her new sister.

The younger girl dipped her head. "I have always thought that when William had children of his own he would spend every waking moment worrying over them."

It was Elizabeth's turn to blush, and she had to make a conscious effort to not put her hand over her still-flat belly. *You don't even know if there is a child!* she silently scolded herself. "We shall have to make sure he does not stay too serious, won't we?" she asked, smiling calmly to hide the butterflies in her stomach.

What would William be like as a father? More serious than her own father, certainly, but also more likely to guide and nurture. Stern, but understanding, she thought. He had all but raised Georgiana, and that was the impression of her brother that the young lady gave.

The door opened to admit the object of her musing, followed closely by the Colonel. "We missed your company too much to stay away for long," the latter proclaimed, giving them a theatrical bow and causing Georgiana to giggle.

"Georgiana, if you are not too tired I would be delighted to hear you play," Darcy said, looking towards the piano. It was not as fine as the instrument in the music room, but Elizabeth had found it to be better quality than the one she had used at Longbourn.

Georgiana stood immediately and went to the instrument. "Is there anything in particular you would like to hear?" she asked.

"Pick whatever you like," Darcy said, taking Georgiana's vacated seat by Lizzy and giving her a small smile.

"I believe, Mr. Darcy, that you sent your sister away just in order to claim her chair," Elizabeth said just for his ears as Georgiana settled herself and began to play.

"You, Mrs. Darcy, are absolutely right," Darcy said back just as quietly. "Perhaps it is having other people in the house, but I feel that I wasted a month by not claiming every moment of your time for myself when I had the chance. I have looked forward to having Richard and Georgiana here, but now I can think only of being just with you."

She quirked an eyebrow at him. "Soon, Mr. Darcy, soon."

*

The next morning after breakfast, Darcy asked Georgiana for a moment of her time. At Elizabeth's insistence, expressed in private the night before, they returned to the sitting room rather than Darcy's office. "She's bound to be upset by the news," Elizabeth had argued. "At least give it to her in a place where she is usually relaxed. Have you ever called her into your office with that stern face of yours on and given her happy news?"

"I don't have a stern face," Darcy had said, trying to frown at her but not quite managing it. He walked over and kissed her cheek. "You make a good point. The sitting room it is."

Now, as they made their way there from the breakfast room, Lizzy tried her best to focus on the coming conversation rather than the queasy feeling in her stomach that had prevented her from having more than tea for breakfast. Her aunt's words about feeling ill during pregnancy repeated themselves in her mind. Only when she recalled that Lydia might be having similar symptoms—without a loving husband by her side—did she successfully turn her attention from her belly.

"What is it?" Georgiana asked as soon as they stepped into the sitting room, worry written across her face. "It must be bad, for Elizabeth didn't eat or laugh at all this morning. Are you ill?" she asked, turning to Lizzy with beseeching eyes, and a wave of guilt spread over Elizabeth. "Was it the cold?"

Darcy frowned slightly at Elizabeth over Georgiana's shoulder, which she took to mean that he had noticed as well and was worried.

"I am well," she told Georgiana, although she made sure to catch her husband's eye too. "I am simply concerned. You are correct, there is bad news. I will let your brother tell you, though."

Georgiana spun to face Darcy, who gestured towards the group of chairs in the center of the room. Georgiana frowned, but seated herself and waited expectantly for them to do the same, her face showing a mix of apprehension and curiosity.

"Georgie, I am sorry I must tell you any of this, but I think it is information that you need to know," Darcy began.

"Someone is hurt," she said immediately, eyes darting between Darcy and Elizabeth.

Lizzy stood up and reseated herself next to her new sister. "Let him tell you. It will be better when you are not assuming something worse than what it is."

Darcy waited a moment, then said baldly, "It is Mr. Wickham."

Georgiana reached over and clutched Elizabeth's hand. "What has he done?"

"He is dead," Darcy said quietly. "He was killed in a duel that he brought about. Colonel Fitzwilliam brought the news from London."

Georgiana frowned. "He didn't tell me."

"No, he wanted to speak with me first. But I thought that you should know."

"What of Lizzy's sister? Lydia?" Georgina asked suddenly, her eyebrows coming together again.

"My aunt writes that she is doing acceptably," Elizabeth said. "She will likely return home to Longbourn."

"But she was—with him?"

Elizabeth hesitated, then pulled out the letter from her aunt and read the beginning of it aloud, making sure to skip her aunt's thoughts on Wickham's character and her worries about Lydia's potential pregnancy. Such a concern was not suitable for an unmarried young lady.

"Poor Lydia," Georgiana said after a pause. Darcy frowned, and seeing it, his sister continued. "He can be so wonderful and convincing and dashing when he wants to be. Of course she fell for his tricks, and now she is alone and frightened and in such an uncertain place in life." She looked down, and for a moment Elizabeth worried that she was going to cry. But when Georgiana looked back up at Darcy, her eyes were full of fire. "May I write to her?"

Elizabeth reacted first. "Georgiana, my sister is perhaps not as innocent as you would believe her to be. She had a good idea of the situation she was getting into and chose that path anyway. And I am not certain she would welcome a letter from you just now."

"I would still like to try," Georgiana said. "It may not help her, but I think that being able to correspond with someone who understands how Wickham can be might help me."

"If you put in writing what he did to you, you never know where that information will end up,"

Darcy said, his gaze shifting to Elizabeth. "There are eyes everywhere."

She smiled slightly, knowing he was thinking of how they came to be married, as Georgiana assured her brother that she would be discreet, and write only of having known Wickham and cared for him when she was much younger.

Darcy agreed, and Georgiana went immediately to the desk that Elizabeth often used to begin her letter. Seeing her settled, Elizabeth turned to her husband. "William, would you be so kind as to escort me to my rooms? As Georgiana noted earlier, my worry left me feeling quite unwell, and I should like to rest."

He stood immediately and helped her stand, plainly worried. "Of course. Georgiana, will you be alright?"

She looked over, clearly concerned as well. "Yes, I am fine. I do hope you feel better soon, Lizzy."

Elizabeth smiled, but said nothing until she and Darcy were in the hallway and out of earshot. "I did not want to worry her more, but it is my stomach that kept me from eating. No, no, don't you worry either," she added quickly. "I—my aunt mentioned that such symptoms occur—" she colored and looked down, wondering how much worse it would be to speak of a pregnancy to anyone other than her husband.

"I see," Darcy said, tipping her chin up and smiling at her, although the worry did not leave his eyes. "Is it very bad?"

"No, I am fine, really. I simply feel queasy, and I am rather tired."

Darcy tucked an arm around her and they continued to her rooms. "Then you must rest, and I will tell the cook to prepare whatever you can bring yourself to eat. You must keep your strength up, Lizzy."

She leaned into him slightly. "You will spoil me, Mr. Darcy."

"I have you as my example," he said. "You nursed your sister most religiously when she was ill at Netherfield, and I will do no less for you."

Elizabeth laughed softly. "Dear Jane! Who could have done less for her? You have on your hands a much less cooperative, compliant patient."

"I would not take any other patient for the world," Darcy told her, opening the door to her rooms and following her in. "And what does my patient mean to do?"

"I really would like to rest," Elizabeth said, "although I do not think I can sleep at the moment. Perhaps I will feel better laying down."

Darcy hesitated, thinking. "Would you like me to read to you?"

She looked at him sheepishly. "Will you think me horribly inconvenient if I say that sounds wonderful?"

He leaned forward and kissed her forehead, then bent farther to capture her mouth. "Dearest, I would be delighted to stay with you. There is nothing I would not do for you, convenient or not." His hand dropped to graze her stomach. "Or for this little one, who is being quite inconvenient by causing his mother discomfort."

"I am afraid we have indeed upset your well-ordered life," Elizabeth said as she removed her shoes. "William?"

"Yes, my love?"

She paused, not certain of how to say what was on her mind. Finally, she said, "I am so lucky, to be here with you. I keep thinking that Lydia—she has none of this. I cannot help but wonder if she is dealing with the same 'illness' that I am. And she is my sister. I worry for her."

Darcy followed her to the bed, pulling a chair close and picking up the book from her bedside table. "All will be well, Elizabeth. Lydia, Georgiana, all of your other sisters, we will make sure that they are cared for. But right now, you need to rest. Let me take care of you, and we can help them once you are feeling better."

Elizabeth nestled into her pillows. "You go to a lot of work for someone who is barely tolerable," she said, giving her husband a sleepy grin.

Darcy brushed a strand of hair off of her face. "You, my exquisitely lovely wife, are more than worth it."

EPILOGUE

Five Years Later

Laughter floated across Pemberley's lawn as two children chased each other towards the approaching phaeton. Elizabeth's dog Nyx ran and jumped alongside of them, adding an occasional bark to the mix.

Inside the phaeton, Elizabeth pulled on the reins to slow the ponies to a walk.

"They certainly are high-energy," Mrs. Gardiner mused. "It is good they can entertain each other, or I think they would drive you mad in a fortnight."

Lizzy laughed. "It helps that they distract each other, and when I fear they are getting close to stealing my sanity I try to slip away for a drive or a ride with Darcy. Your idea of a phaeton and a pair was ingenious, and I am glad you were able to join me today!"

Mrs. Gardiner smiled. "With the children older, it has gotten easier to be away from home for a while. It gives Julia practice managing the household, and I must say she has done a remarkable job in the past."

The children were close enough now that Elizabeth could clearly make out the calls of "Mama, mama!" and "Wait for us!" Stopping the ponies, she helped her daughter Anne climb up while Mrs. Gardiner assisted little George.

"It's lucky that you two are still small," Mrs. Gardiner told them. "I don't think all of us will fit in here once you're grown up."

"I won't ride in carriages when I'm big!" George proclaimed, bouncing up and down. "I'll have a giant black stallion like Uncle Darcy and we'll gallop everywhere we go!"

"Mama, can I drive?" Anne asked as Elizabeth settled the girl on her lap.

"You can hold onto the reins just in front of my hands, but don't pull," Elizabeth said. Once Anne's small hands had found their place, Elizabeth clucked to the ponies and they finished the short drive to the stables, where stable hands came out to take charge of the ponies and phaeton.

"I forgot to tell you, I just had a letter from Jane," Lizzy told her aunt over the children's chatter as they walked back down the incline to the house. "She writes that baby Emma is doing well, and little Charles has resigned himself to having a sister. They hope to come for a visit later this summer. I am supposed to pass on her regards; Jane wished she could see you while you were here, but traveling with a newborn is nearly impossible."

"I am simply happy that Jane and Emma are both doing well," Mrs. Gardiner responded. "It must be pleasant having Jane and Mr. Bingley so close now that they bought the new estate."

Elizabeth laughed. "It is wonderful, even though Mama bemoans the fact that they left Netherfield every time I hear from her. I think she blames me for taking them away!"

"Nonsense." Mrs. Gardiner gave her niece a slightly mischievous smile. "Obviously it is the gorgeous Derbyshire landscape that convinced them to leave. I would come back here in a heartbeat if your uncle could leave his business."

"Watch what you say, or I'll find reasons to keep you here forever," Lizzy joked. "No one else has had any luck getting Anne to sit still long enough to learn her letters."

"Yes, stay, stay," Anne exclaimed, catching onto the conversation and taking hold of Mrs. Gardiner's hand to skip beside her. "You can read to me every night!"

"And make us costumes!" George added. "I want another pirate costume!"

The front door opened and Lydia came out, meeting them at the bottom of the steps. "Mama, tell Aunt Gardiner to stay so she can make me another pirate costume," George said, running up to Lydia and bouncing up and down in front of her.

Lydia picked him up and leaned him over backwards until he shrieked to be let up, laughing breathlessly. "But Aunt Gardiner has her own children," she told the now tomato-faced boy. "Would you like it if I went away and didn't come back because another little boy wanted me to stay and play with him?"

George frowned. "Noooo," he said slowly. "But I could stay with Aunt Lizzie until you came back, and Uncle Darcy said he's going to let me ride a pony all on my own!"

"Well, I would miss you very much," Lydia told her son, kissing his nose and setting him back on the ground. "As I am sure that Aunt Gardiner misses her own children."

"They can come stay here!" Anne exclaimed. "Can't they, Mama? We have hundreds and hundreds of rooms!"

"Let it be noted that your child suggested it, not mine," Lydia told Elizabeth with a small smile.

Lizzy stifled her grin. "Let it be noted, Miss Anne, that we only have dozens of rooms. Aunt Gardiner really does have to leave, but perhaps we can persuade her to come back at Christmas time with her family. What would you think about that?"

After a moment of thought, Anne and George both reluctantly agreed to the idea. Winking back at Elizabeth and Mrs. Gardiner, Lydia led the two off to the nursery to change out of their mussed play clothes, leaving the other ladies free to retire to the sitting room.

"I never would have guessed it, but that boy has been the best thing that ever happened to Lydia," Mrs. Gardiner said quietly once they were out of earshot. "She is steadier and more responsible than I ever thought to see her—and she seems happy, too. I love your mother, but it is good for Lydia that she managed to develop her personality beyond Fannie's influence."

"Darcy and I had low hopes when we suggested she come and stay with us," Elizabeth admitted in the same low tone. "The first few months had some rough patches, but Lydia has been full of pleasant surprises. She is wonderful with the children, which is quite a relief for me sometimes." She rested her hand briefly on a swelling belly still mostly concealed by her gown. "With Richard walking and Anne running headlong into everything, the nurse and I have both had our hands full on occasion. I'm honestly not sure what I'd do without Lydia at this point, especially when I have to go into confinement."

"What does Mr. Darcy think of having little George around?" Mrs. Gardiner asked as they entered the sitting room and settled themselves. "I'll admit that I didn't know the older George well, but even I can see the resemblance."

Elizabeth hesitated, thinking. "It was harder for Darcy, at first, and still is now when he does something particularly similar to his father," she said slowly. "For the most part, I think he feels as if he was given a second chance—that he knows what not to do wrong this time, and can help little George be a better man that his father was. And I think that in time, little George will appreciate having someone who knew his father as a boy. He doesn't have questions now, but when he does Darcy can answer them far better than Lydia or I ever could."

"And you, Lizzy?" Mrs. Gardiner asked. "Are you happy? Has the dastardly haughty man been treating you well?"

Elizabeth laughed lightly, her hand returning to the swell of her stomach again and remembering her husband's joy when she had told him she was expecting their third child. She thought of Darcy's daily visits to the nursery, their rides together—for she had finally learned to enjoy horses—and how he had presented Nyx to her as a puppy after the old hunting dog Orion had died so that she would always have a companion for her walks. She thought of how he treated little George Wickham, a boy he had every reason to hate, as he treated his own son. Elizabeth Darcy had no doubts that her husband was the absolute best of men.

"Oh yes, Aunt," she said with a wide smile. "I have never been happier."

ABOUT THE AUTHOR

Jennifer Kay has loved historical fiction since she was first introduced to Little House on the Prairie. When she ran out of books to read, Jennifer began writing her own. She considers it fitting that Pride and Prejudice, one of history's keystone novels, should be the basis for her first published book, *Before a Fall*.

Made in the USA
Lexington, KY
20 May 2019